THE SUBMARINE CAPER

THE HARDY BOYS® MYSTERY STORIES

THE
SUBMARINE
CAPER

Franklin W. Dixon

Illustrated by Leslie Morrill

WANDERER BOOKS
Published by Simon & Schuster, New York

Published by WANDERER BOOKS
A Simon & Schuster Division of
Gulf & Western Corporation
Simon & Schuster Building
1230 Avenue of the Americas
New York, New York 10020

Manufactured in the United States of America
10 9 8 7 6 5 4 3 2 1

WANDERER and colophon are trademarks of Simon & Schuster
THE HARDY BOYS is a trademark of Stratemeyer Syndicate,
registered in the United States Patent and Trademark Office

Library of Congress Cataloging in Publication Data
Dixon, Franklin W.
The submarine caper
(The Hardy boys mystery stories; 68)
Summary: On a visit to Germany the Hardy brothers
investigate the theft of plans for a newly invented
submarine and the mysterious disappearance of
valuable coins and paintings.
[1. Mystery and detective stories. 2. Germany—
Fiction] I. Title. II. Series: Dixon, Franklin W.
Hardy boys mystery stories.
PZ7.D644Sv   [Fic]   81–3361
ISBN   0–671–42338–X   AACR2
ISBN 0–671–42339–8 (pbk.)

Contents

1	*Surprise Collision*	7
2	*Danger on the Autobahn*	13
3	*A Mysterious Clue*	23
4	Taler, Taler	32
5	*The Ransacked Room*	40
6	*Futile Chase*	47
7	*A Horrible Discovery*	56
8	*Two Hunches*	62
9	*News at Maria's*	72
10	*A Bird Flies Away*	79
11	*A Trap!*	89
12	*A Surprising Development*	97
13	*The Man in the Lobby*	105
14	*A Telltale Initial*	114
15	*A Late-Night Row*	124
16	*A Violent Fight*	132
17	*Underwater Danger*	142
18	*Hunt for a Truck*	155
19	*The Secret of Bear Lake*	165
20	*Amphibian Arrest*	178

1 Surprise Collision

"Remember my friend Alfred Wagner?" Gerhard Stolz asked Frank and Joe Hardy, who were staying at his Munich apartment. "You met him when I took you to his auto repair shop a few weeks ago. He's got a serious problem."

"What happened?" Joe asked. "Is *Ludwig II* giving him headaches?" He was referring to the mini-submarine Wagner had invented and was building in his spare time. It was named after the inventor's favorite king, which resulted in plenty of teasing from his friends.

"No. *Ludwig II* is fine—in fact, it'll have its maiden run next week," Gerhard replied. He was a

7

slender man of medium height, who now creased his forehead into a thoughtful frown.

Frank looked at him questioningly. "What is it then?"

"Wagner is afraid that someone has copied the blueprint for his sub."

Frank whistled. "That would be very serious, indeed. What makes him think his plans were duplicated?"

"He found an empty film container under his desk and put two and two together, even though he can't prove it. I went to see him last night because my battery needed to be recharged. That's when he told me someone was after his sub. He had noticed a while ago that his papers had been disturbed. After that, he locked them into a drawer, but he says it happened again."

"Are you sure he's not imagining things?" Joe inquired.

"I doubt it. He's a very trusting person and it takes a lot to rouse his suspicion." Gerhard Stolz poured himself a second cup of breakfast coffee.

"I promised Alfred I'd look into the matter," he added.

Stolz was a well-known investigative reporter who had met Frank and Joe's father, a famous New York detective, many years ago. The two had become good friends, and when he heard that the boys wanted to spend a summer in Germany to sightsee and brush up on their language skills, he invited them to stay with him and his wife Rita. Eighteen-year-old Frank and his brother, who was a year younger, were accomplished amateur detectives themselves, and found Stolz's work fascinating.

Frank was about to ask Gerhard whether Wagner suspected anyone in particular, when the phone rang. He picked it up and after listening for a moment, handed it to Gerhard. "It's your paper, the *Herold*."

"Oh, thanks. I'll take it in my study."

Frank waited until Stolz picked up the extension, and then quietly hung up. He flopped into a chair and grinned at his brother. "Your turn to do the dishes today!"

Joe grimaced. "I was hoping you'd forget." He cleaned the table and was just about finished with his chore when Gerhard rushed back into the kitchen.

"Boys, would you do me a favor?" he asked. "I have to catch a ten o'clock flight to Frankfurt. Would you drop me off at the airport?"

"Sure," Frank said. "What's up?"

"Tell you on the way. Go ahead and start the car. I'll be right down."

While Stolz hurried into the bedroom to pack a

few things, the two boys left the apartment. They did not wait for the elevator, but ran down the stairs into the garage. Gerhard owned a blue Mercedes, the car he usually drove, and a silver-gray Porsche, which he loaned the boys during their visit.

Frank slipped behind the wheel of the Mercedes, while his blond brother climbed into the back. Then they drove around to the front door and waited until Gerhard arrived with his suitcase and joined them.

"Why is the paper sending you to Frankfurt?" Joe asked eagerly. "Do you have to investigate an interesting case?"

Gerhard smiled. "No. I'm only going there because my final destination, the little town of Glocken on the Rhine River, has no airport."

He told the boys that in Glocken a number of priceless paintings had been hidden during World War II and could not be found afterwards. Now the hiding place had been discovered by accident, and the townspeople were planning a festive ceremony, in which the paintings were to be removed from the hiding place and escorted to the museum.

"That's all I know," Stolz said. "I was asked to cover the story, and accepted because it won't take much time. Besides, I'm getting a nice weekend trip to the Rhine."

"Look at him!" Frank grinned at their friend, while he pushed a strand of dark hair off his forehead. "Goes off on a fun weekend and leaves his company home!"

Gerhard laughed. "Well, it's not quite like that. I have to do some work, and you'll hardly die of boredom in Munich. You two always find something to keep you busy."

"We were counting on you to take us to the movies!" Joe protested.

"Tell you what," Gerhard said, suddenly serious. "Why don't you drop by Alfred Wagner's and see if anything new has developed?"

"We'll be glad to," Frank offered.

"Great. And mention to him why I couldn't make it myself. I'm sure he'll understand."

"Business first," Joe said with a chuckle.

Gerhard made a face. "I do have to earn a living."

"How about Rita?" Joe asked. "Does she know about your trip?"

The journalist slapped his hand against his forehead. "Oh, I forgot to leave her a note! Please tell her what happened, will you? I'll be back Sunday night."

"You'd better bring her some flowers," Frank advised his friend. "Maybe then she'll forgive you for rushing off like this."

"Good idea!"

After Gerhard Stolz boarded his flight, Frank and

Joe drove directly to Alfred Wagner's. The inventor's garage was located on the outskirts of town next to a small lake, which he used for the experimental runs of his sub. Adjoining his repair shop was a charming old frame house where he lived with his mother and sister.

Frank parked the Mercedes behind a red Alfa Romeo.

"Oh, look at that beautiful car!" Joe exclaimed. "I'd love to have a set of wheels like that."

"So would I," Frank agreed, as the boys got out. They admiringly surveyed the elegant sports car before entering the large, noisy shop. They walked in between cars with open hoods, and past half a dozen mechanics who were working on them.

"*Guten Tag,*" several of the men smiled in greeting as the visitors made their way to the end of the shop, where a small wooden cubicle served as Wagner's office.

The boys had almost reached it when the door flew open and a young girl stormed out. She collided head-on with Joe, who was standing right in her path!

2 *Danger on the Autobahn*

The girl glared at Joe, who mumbled an apology. Still looking angry, she hurried away, her long blond hair bouncing as she moved

"How do you like that?" Joe asked, looking after her. "I wonder what's bugging her?"

Just then, an impatient voice sounded from behind. "What are you doing here?"

The Hardys whirled around and faced a short, wiry man with a head of unruly dark hair and metal-rimmed glasses. He was Alfred Wagner.

When he recognized them, his tense expression dissolved into a smile. "Oh, it's you, boys," he said. "Sorry I shouted, but I'm beginning to get suspicious of everyone. Did you hear the story about my drawings?"

"Yes," Joe confirmed. "That's why we're here. But what was wrong with that pretty girl? She almost ran me over."

Wagner shrugged. "Who knows? Anyway, she was too nosy for me. Said she was a reporter, but I didn't believe her and told her to leave."

"Good for you," Frank said.

"Why don't you come into my office?" Wagner suggested. "It's tiny, but nicer than out here in the shop."

The brothers followed him into the small room. Papers and drawings were strewn all over and folders lay on the floor. Here Wagner worked on his many inventions, which he enjoyed far more than running the car repair business he had inherited from his father.

Frank told him about Gerhard Stolz's trip and asked Wagner if he had an idea of who might have copied his plans for the mini-sub.

"I don't like to suspect anyone," Wagner replied. "For years, I've been leaving my papers in here and no one has touched them. Now I have to lock them up, and even that doesn't seem to help."

"Perhaps you should invent a safe that can't be cracked!" Joe grinned.

"You're right. But first I'll have to complete my sub. Come on, I'll show it to you."

Wagner led the boys to a shack next to the garage. At the far wall, a rising door opened up to the lakefront. On a rack near the door was the yellow mini-sub. It was about twenty-one feet long, six feet high, and was shaped somewhat like a turtle. It could be lowered by means of a winch into a narrow canal of water and driven right out of the shack into the lake.

A young man in overalls was climbing out of the hatch with a wrench in his hand. Wagner introduced him as his assistant, Rolf Meier.

"We'll just have to modify a few things," the inventor told his visitors proudly. "But *Ludwig II* should be ready for its first test run in a week or two. If you want, you can come along."

"Great!" the boys cried in unison, and Frank added, "Just think, Joe, of all the things that little sub can do! We can go a lot deeper with it than with our diving suits."

"Yes, to about fifteen hundred feet," Wagner said. "But not in this puddle. All we have here is a depth of sixty or seventy feet, with mud, algae, and garbage at the bottom."

He locked the shack and invited the boys to his house for coffee and cake. They met his mother and

sister, then everyone sat down on the patio, where Frau Wagner served freshly baked *Apfelkuchen.*

As Frank helped himself to a second piece of the delicious apple cake, he asked, "Herr Wagner, I understand there are various mini-subs on the market. Do you have any idea why someone wants *yours* so badly that he'll resort to a criminal act?"

"I've asked myself the same question," Wagner replied. "My invention contains only a few improvements over the others. The reason must be that *Ludwig II* is very inexpensive compared to other boats of its size and capacity."

"How come?" Joe asked.

"It's made of fiberglass. The special shape of the body makes it possible to avoid using steel, which is heavier and costlier."

"Are you planning to build more of these boats if the test run is successful?" Frank asked.

"No, I'm not interested in that. I want to sell the license to a large manufacturer. The manager is a friend of mine, and we already wrote up a contract."

"Then it must be the competition who's trying to steal your plans," Frank declared. "Once your friend begins to market these subs for a low price, other manufacturers will be in trouble."

Everyone agreed that this made sense. Then Joe inquired as to how the culprit had been able to get to Wagner's drawings.

"Unfortunately, that was no problem," the inventor admitted. "I have simple locks on my office door and my desk drawers. And I'm really not sure who has the keys to what locks. That's why I think the spy might be one of my employees." Wagner looked unhappy at the thought.

"Would anyone have a chance to sneak into your office, perhaps at lunchtime?" Joe asked.

"No, too many people are around then. But often one of the men will stay late, and at that hour, Meier and I usually work in the shack. The person could easily walk into my office unobserved, or even come during the night, for that matter. I do know several mechanics have their own keys to the shop. I'm just not sure what other keys they might have."

After thanking the Wagners for their hospitality, Frank and Joe drove back to Gerhard's apartment. Rita Stolz heard them coming and opened the door. She was a slender, pretty woman with short, reddish hair.

"I'm glad you're here," she greeted them. "Gerhard just called a minute ago. He wants you to join him in Glocken."

"In Glocken?" Joe exclaimed, puzzled. "I wonder why?"

"I have no idea," Rita replied. "He didn't give me

any details. Just said he needed you by tomorrow noon, and it would be best if you could leave now and get there before morning."

"Looks as if his nice, pleasant weekend was just a dream," Joe said with a grin, as the Hardys began to pack a few things. "I'm sure he has a problem or he wouldn't have called for us."

Soon the boys were on their way with Joe driving. Traffic was heavy until they reached the Autobahn to Nuremberg. From then on, they whizzed along at top speed. They changed places at a rest area, and Frank took the wheel. But they hit heavy traffic once more, and by the time they could move freely again, it was already dark.

Another car was behind them and stuck like glue. Its headlights irritated Frank, causing him to say angrily, "One more inch and that guy'll hit our trunk!" The boy moved into the right lane to let the car pass. The driver pulled up, but when he was about parallel with the Hardys, he pushed toward the right lane, getting perilously close to the young detectives.

"That crazy idiot!" Frank cried. "He's cutting us off!"

They were forced further and further to the right. Finally, Frank braked hard in order to avoid driving onto the shoulder. The Porsche started to fishtail and turned around almost 360 degrees! Finally, it stopped with screeching tires.

Their knees shaking, the boys climbed out and pushed the car to the side. The other driver was nowhere in sight by now.

"Wow!" Frank wiped the perspiration off his forehead. "Did you ever see anything like this?"

"That lady was out of her mind," Joe agreed, as he walked around the Porsche to check if there was any damage. Luckily, everything seemed to be in order.

"Lady?" Frank asked. "I only noticed the red sports car. I didn't see the driver."

"I couldn't swear to it, but I think it was a woman with long blond hair," Joe said. "Well, at least nothing happened." He took the wheel again, and passed Frankfurt. Finally, he turned off the Autobahn to drive along the Rhine River. They arrived at their destination late at night. The Hotel Glockenhof was in the picturesque town square. Joe parked across the street since the parking lot was full.

"We'd better leave our things in the car till we're sure they have a room for us," Frank said, and the two boys walked into the lobby. They asked for Gerhard Stolz and were directed into the dining room, where the reporter was talking to Herr Dietrich, the owner of the hotel.

Stolz greeted them with a friendly smile, introduced them to Herr Dietrich, then ordered something for them to eat. Much to their relief, the kitchen was still open.

"How was your trip?" Gerhard inquired.

"Don't ask. We almost got run off the road," Joe replied, and described the incident on the Autobahn. However, when a huge platter with salads and cold cuts arrived, the boys did not let the recollection spoil their appetite. They dug in with gusto.

Then Joe asked why Gerhard had called for them.

"It's a long story, and we'd better go to bed now," Gerhard replied. "Tomorrow morning we'll have plenty of time. The festivities don't start till early afternoon. We can do some sightseeing and I'll tell you what's happening, okay?"

"Seems we have no choice," Frank replied with a grin. "But I have to admit, I could use some sleep."

"I reserved a room for you," Gerhard said. "It's right next to mine."

The boys went outside to get their luggage. They had only gone a few steps when Frank called out, "Joe! Look over there!"

His brother stopped short and saw a shadowy figure tiptoe away from the Porsche and disappear around the corner. Quickly, Joe chased after Frank, who had already started to pursue the stranger.

Suddenly, Joe heard a yell. Flying around the corner, he ran straight into someone who was just getting up from the ground. The two crashed to the sidewalk!

3 A Mysterious Clue

"Hey!" Frank sputtered and clutched his right side in pain. "Can't you watch where you're going?"

Joe scrambled to his feet. "How was I supposed to know you were sitting around the bend letting that man escape?"

"Listen to this! First I get knocked on the head by some creep, then you come along and run me over, and to top it all off, you yell at me!"

"When you're finished complaining," Joe said with a grin, "why don't you tell me what happened?"

Just then the boys heard footsteps, and the next moment, Gerhard Stolz walked around the corner. "Here you are!" he called out. "I saw you running off and couldn't figure out what was going on."

"We noticed someone tampering with the car," Frank replied. "I think he had a tiny flashlight. Anyway, when he saw us coming, he ran off. I caught up to him and grabbed him by his jacket, but he punched me in the head and took off."

"What did the man look like?" Gerhard asked.

"Couldn't see much," Frank admitted. "Not enough light. But he was young, and dark-haired. I think he wore a mustache. But I doubt that I'd recognize him in daylight."

"Let's check the car and see if he did any damage," Gerhard suggested, and the three returned to the Porsche. A short inspection revealed that nothing was missing.

"We'll drive into the lot now," Frank suggested. "It has emptied out a bit."

He and Gerhard climbed into the Porsche. Just before Joe got in, he noticed a handkerchief a few feet away. Thinking it might have something to do with the stranger, he picked it up and put it in his pocket, making a mental note to study it in the morning. Then, anxious for some rest, Joe squeezed into the car, every muscle in his body aching. Frank drove into the hotel lot, and the boys took their suitcases to their room.

Completely exhausted, they fell into bed. Next

day after breakfast, Gerhard asked the hotel chef to pack a lunch for them. The three walked through the quaint old town into the vineyards that rose up directly behind Glocken.

As they climbed up the vine-covered mountain in the early morning sunshine, Frank said, "Gerhard, I can't wait any longer. Won't you tell us why you wanted us to join you?"

"I will. But first let me bring you up-to-date on what I learned from Mayor Reimann about those paintings. You see, there's a little museum in Glocken containing old documents, woodcuts, tools, and furniture, the usual local antiques. Before World War II, however, the museum owned a veritable treasure—five very valuable paintings by the Sexton."

"The Sexton?" Frank asked. "Who's that?"

"A medieval painter. His name is unknown, but apparently he was the sexton in this town. He never signed his pictures but marked them with a little bell. He is said to have painted eight masterworks and five of them were here in the museum."

"I bet those paintings are worth a fortune!" Joe exclaimed.

"Oh, yes, a few million dollars," Gerhard replied.

"What happened to them?" Frank asked.

"They were put away during the war," Gerhard

answered. "But unfortunately they were hidden so well that afterward no one could find them. All people knew was that Mayor Altenberg and three other men took the paintings to a secret place one night."

"And those men didn't remember where they put them?" Joe asked.

"All four died. For years, the town and the surrounding area were searched systematically, but the treasure was never found."

"Apparently, it has been found now," Joe said. "How come? Did the old mayor visit the new mayor in his dreams and tell him about the hiding place?"

Stolz grinned. "No, nothing that far out. The daughter of Mayor Altenberg cleaned up her father's library and found a piece of paper in an old volume. The note was in her father's handwriting and revealed the hiding place."

"Where is it?" Frank asked eagerly.

"In the wine cellar of his home. From there, a secret door leads to a room in which stands a huge wooden chest. The paintings were placed inside after being packed in a waterproof metal container."

"Mysterious notes and secret doors," Joe said. "Sounds like a great mystery!"

Gerhard nodded. "And the paintings aren't the only things that were hidden," he went on.

"What else?" Joe asked eagerly.

26

"A collection of gold coins called *Joachimstaler*. It belonged to the former mayor of Glocken."

The three stopped and rested for a moment, turning around to look at the town. Talk of the missing paintings and coins ceased abruptly.

"Oh, what a view!" Joe cried out. "Wait till I take a picture!" He pulled out his camera, adjusted the setting, and looked through the viewfinder. "It's dusty," he said, pulling a handkerchief out of his pocket. "What's this—" He stared at the handkerchief, then let out a low whistle.

Frank and Gerhard looked at him in surprise.

"I almost forgot!" Joe cried out. "This handkerchief may belong to the guy who sneaked around our car last night. I picked it up from the street, but I was so tired that I just put it in my pocket and forgot about it."

Gerhard examined the silk handkerchief. "What an unusual pattern," he said, "light blue stripes with something like suns in between them. They have long rays and faces. Strange."

"Somehow this pattern rings a bell," Frank said. "Maybe I'll remember later what it reminds me of."

The group continued on and Joe said, "Now we know all about the paintings and the coins, but you still haven't told us why we were supposed to come to Glocken, Gerhard."

"I received an anonymous phone call yesterday,"

Stolz explained. "A man said, 'You'll be in for a surprise when the hiding place is opened tomorrow!'"

"A surprise!" Frank repeated. "Do you know what he means by that?"

"I haven't the vaguest idea. In a few hours we'll know more. I have a hunch there'll be trouble, that's why I called you. Things like that are right up your alley, aren't they?"

"You bet!" Frank grinned. "But suppose it was just a practical joker who phoned you?"

"I think there's more to it than that. Why would he call me, of all people? Anyway, I have to go back to Munich tomorrow afternoon. If there's a mystery to be solved, will you take over?"

"We'll be glad to," Frank replied with a grin. "Besides, it's so nice here we wouldn't mind spending a few days, would we, Joe?"

Joe agreed, then suggested they stop for lunch.

"By the way," Gerhard said, after taking a big bite out of his sandwich, "did you get a chance to talk to Alfred Wagner yesterday?"

"We sure did," Frank said and repeated in detail what happened. With a grin, he mentioned the young lady whom Wagner had asked to leave his shop. Suddenly, Joe held up his hand.

"Frank! The Alfa Romeo!" he sputtered. "Remember it wasn't there when we left Alfred's place?"

Frank realized what his brother was getting at. "You're right! I had a hunch that the incident on the Autobahn was no coincidence! She must have pushed us over on purpose!"

"What are you talking about?" Gerhard wanted to know.

"Remember, we almost got killed yesterday by a blond girl in a red sports car," Joe replied. "And now I recall that in front of Wagner's garage there was this red sports car—an Alfa Romeo!"

"Our attacker and the girl might have been one and the same person!" Frank added.

"But why would she do a thing like that?"

"Maybe to scare us. She's no reporter. She probably belongs to the group who copied Wagner's drawings! She could be working with one of his employees."

"You've got a point there," Gerhard had to admit. On the way back to town, the three discussed Wagner's problems and his suspicion that the culprit might be one of his mechanics.

"We'll have to check all of them out," Frank decided. "Starting with Alfred's assistant, Rolf Meier."

The trio returned from the vineyards and soon

found themselves in front of the mansionlike home of the former Mayor, Helmut Altenberg, which was located in a small valley outside of town. Between the house and the wine cellar, which was built into a hill, was a wide yard. It was now full of gaily chattering people. Flags flew in the wind, a brass band and a school choir were ready to perform. The festivities had just begun.

Gerhard and the Hardys made their way through the crowd and joined a group of reporters who were led down into the wine cellar by a guide.

In the dark, cool room, Mayor Reimann greeted the people from the press and introduced the honorary guests—government representatives, the city council, members of the state assembly, and, of course, Doris Altenberg, a trim, dark-haired woman with a friendly face, who held her father's letter in her hand.

"Here at the end of the cellar," Reimann declared, "you see the bottom of a keg built into the wall. It's five feet high and seems to be merely a decoration. However, from the note, we learned that it is really a door to another room. Fräulein Altenberg will now open it according to the directions her father left behind."

As the woman stepped toward the wall and counted the boards, everyone stood in silent anticipation. Then Doris Altenberg pressed a certain spot and the heavy oak door sprang open!

Large spotlights had been set up and were now directed into the secret room. It was empty, except for a wooden chest in the middle. Tension was high as the woman walked over to it, opened the lid, and looked inside.

Suddenly, Doris Altenberg turned pale and let the lid fall in its place. "It's empty!" she whispered. "There's nothing in this chest!"

4 Taler, Taler

There was a stunned silence at first, then a storm seemed to break loose. Shouting and gesticulating angrily, the guests pushed toward the wooden chest to look inside.

A government representative turned to the mayor. "If this is supposed to be a joke, I don't get it!" he snarled.

"Did *you* fake the note, or did Fräulein Altenberg?" another man cried out.

"Why don't you admit that you arranged this whole thing just to get some free publicity for your tourist trade?" a reporter commented snidely.

The beleaguered mayor denied the accusations vehemently. "You had better watch what you're saying!" he cried out. "We have expert testimony that this note is, indeed, written by Mayor Altenberg!"

Doris Altenberg, who had been standing frozen in utter shock, began to defend her father and protested loudly against any allegations of forgery.

The news spread quickly to the crowd outside, and people began pushing into the cellar, blocking the entrance. Finally, Reimann managed to be heard above the unruly mob.

"Please leave immediately," he called out. "The ceremony is herewith canceled. I'll make sure that the matter will be investigated properly."

With the help of the local police, he managed to evacuate the cellar and persuade people to go home. Gerhard, Frank, and Joe realized immediately that this was the surprise the anonymous caller had been hinting at. They surveyed the room carefully. It was smaller than the wine cellar, and the back wall had crumbled. Now a mountain of debris formed the end of the room.

"Once this must have been a section of the wine cellar," Gerhard said. "Then part of it caved in, and they just built a new wall and put in a secret door."

When everyone had left, Mayor Reimann asked Gerhard Stolz if he could help him clear up the mystery. "Of course, the police will be working on the case, too," the mayor assured him. "But with your experience as an investigative reporter, you might be able to uncover a clue."

"I'm sorry," Gerhard replied, "I have to return to Munich tomorrow. But my two young friends will be glad to assist you." He introduced Frank and Joe and told the mayor about the many mysteries they had solved in their own country.

Reimann accepted the offer and assured Frank and Joe of his full cooperation.

At dinner that night, Gerhard and the boys discussed the mystery. "I wonder if Altenberg himself was the thief," Joe spoke up. "Of course then he wouldn't have written that note."

"I think his daughter is innocent, too," Frank added. "Otherwise, she would've destroyed the letter."

"Before we come to any conclusions," Gerhard said, "we'll have to find the answer to a number of questions. Let's assume the pictures and the coins were in the same container. When was it stolen? Who had the opportunity to take it? How could it have been removed from the cellar without anyone noticing?"

"Also, someone knew ahead of time that the pictures and the coins weren't there," Frank said. "The anonymous caller. Who's he and how did he know?"

"And what was he after?" Joe added. "Is he involved with the paintings, coins, or both? We should find out more about the gold *Joachimstaler*, too."

"Wait a minute," Gerhard said and stood up. "I'll be right back."

When he returned, he smiled. "I just phoned a well-known coin dealer in Frankfurt who's a friend of mine. He'll see us tomorrow at noon, even though it's Sunday."

The following day, the three detectives parked the Porsche in front of the coin dealer's home. Joe, who had squeezed into the narrow back seat, stretched and complained about being stiff before ringing the doorbell. Lothar Rehm, a tall man with white hair and thick eyeglasses, greeted the visitors and led them into his study on the second floor.

"Well, Gerhard, what mystery are you working on this time?" he asked with a smile.

Gerhard explained their mission, and the dealer looked thoughtful. "That's strange, indeed," he said. "You see, *Joachimstaler* or *Schlicktaler* are really silver coins that were minted in the Joachimstal in Bohemia in the sixteenth century."

"Is that why they're called *Taler*?" Frank asked.

"Right. The coins became so popular that they spread throughout the country and Europe. Via Spain, the *Taler* was brought to America—"

35

"And that's where it was called 'dollar!' " Joe put in.

"That's correct. But let's get back to the *Joachimstaler*. Count Stephan von Schlick, who ran the mint, had a couple of hundred gold coins made around 1520. Those were not intended as currency. Instead, he used them as gifts for royalty such as Emperor Karl V and King Ludwig I of Bohemia."

"That makes them very valuable, I suppose," Gerhard Stolz put in.

"It depends on their condition. A collector may pay between a thousand and four thousand dollars for one. There are four editions of the gold *Joachimstaler*, with slight variations only an expert can detect. If you have all four, they increase in value."

"Do you have any?" Frank asked.

"No. But I can show you a picture." The dealer took a large volume from a bookshelf. "Here's one. On one side there is the holy Joachim with the Schlick family's coat of arms at his feet, and on the other side stands the Bohemian lion with its oddly stylized double tail."

The three visitors studied the picture and memorized each detail of the coin. Finally, Gerhard spoke up. "Lothar, has anyone ever come in here to sell you gold *Joachimstaler*?"

The dealer wrinkled his forehead. "Not that I

remember. But strangely enough, someone visited me just the other day and asked if I had *bought* any of the coins recently, and from whom. Of course, I didn't tell him anything."

"Do you know his name?" Frank asked.

Herr Rehm shook his head. "I don't think he ever told me."

"Do you remember what he looked like?"

"Yes. He was around fifty, short and heavyset, with a round face and bald head. Wore a light tan suit. And I noticed another thing. Part of his left ring-finger was missing."

"That's a great description, Herr Rehm," Joe said. "I'm sure this man is connected with our case."

"Lothar," Gerhard said thoughtfully, "would you give *us* the information you refused him?"

"Sure," the dealer replied. "I don't mind telling you. Let me run downstairs and check."

When Herr Rehm returned, he was shaking his head. "I only bought three gold *Joachimstaler* in the last ten years," he reported, "and all of them from other dealers. I acquired them for customers whom I have personally known for a long time."

"If you think of anything else that might help us," Frank said, "please call us at the Glockenhof in Glocken."

The dealer promised to do so; the visitors thanked him for his help and then left. Frank and Joe drove Gerhard to the Frankfurt airport and, while they waited for the boarding announcement, discussed the case.

"If somebody found the metal container and sold the coins," Frank said, "he could have gone to a different dealer. Matter of fact, he could have sold them anywhere in the world!"

Gerhard nodded. "I'll try to check with other dealers in the country, at least."

"And the guy who wanted to know if Herr Rehm sold any coins," Joe said. "How does he fit into our case?"

"He may suspect that the container was found and the coins were sold, and he wanted to find out by whom," Frank replied.

Gerhard agreed. "In any case, your next step should be to find out as much about the paintings as you can, and to search the secret cellar closely. Maybe you'll get an idea how the paintings and the coins could have been removed."

A few minutes later, Stolz boarded his flight for Munich, and the boys drove back to the quaint town on the Rhine River.

When Frank put the key into the lock of their hotel room, it would not turn. "That's funny," he said. "I could have sworn I locked up." He opened the door, stepped inside, and gasped.

The room was a mess! Drawers had been pulled out, the closet door stood open, and their things were strewn all over the place!

5 The Ransacked Room

Joe, who was looking over his brother's shoulder, whistled. "We had a visitor!"

"Seems he did a thorough job of ripping everything apart!" Frank fumed. "Come on, let's see if he left a clue."

Carefully, he examined the doorknob, the handles on the drawers, and pieces of furniture for fingerprints. "Nothing." He sighed. "Our visitor was a pro. I wonder how he got in."

Joe walked to the hall door, checked the lock from the outside, and discovered a few scratches.

"Forced entry," he declared dryly. "Well, I guess we have no choice but to clean up. At least that'll tell us if anything's missing."

Grumbling, the boys began to straighten up.

They found that Joe's old camera had disappeared.

"Luckily, I didn't leave the new one in our room," the boy declared. "The old camera wasn't worth much. I don't even know why I brought it with me."

"Perhaps the thief only swiped it because he couldn't find what he was really after," Frank spoke up.

"What do you mean?"

"Do you still have that handkerchief you found near our car?"

Joe opened a bureau drawer. "Oh, no!" he cried out. "I put it in here, but it's gone! Now I get the message. The intruder came to retrieve the handkerchief and took the camera to make it look like a burglary!"

"Exactly," Frank agreed. "The handkerchief must be very incriminating for him to have gone to all this trouble. If only I could remember where I've seen the pattern!"

Joe nodded. "It looked familiar to me, too. But I don't know the answer."

The boys reported the incident to Herr Dietrich, who was flabbergasted. He wanted to call the police, but Frank persuaded him that since the loss was so small, it was hardly worth it.

"Do you know if any other rooms were broken into?" he asked.

41

"Oh, no. Of course not. One is enough! This is the first time something like this has happened in my hotel!"

"It won't happen again," Frank assured him. "We're convinced that this was not an ordinary thief. He came for a special reason." Quickly, he told Herr Dietrich what had happened the night before. The boys left and were about to cross the lobby when the clerk at the reception desk waved to them.

"You had a phone call this afternoon," he said. "Unfortunately, the man didn't leave his name."

"No wonder," Joe grumbled. "He only called to make sure we weren't in our room. Did he ask for our room number?"

"Well—no. He asked to talk to Mr. Frank Hardy in room 17. I told him you had room 25, and wouldn't be back before late afternoon. Why? Did I say the the wrong thing?"

"No, no," Joe assured him. "Everything's okay."

The boys discussed the strange phone call over dinner that night. "How'd the thief get my name?" Frank wondered.

"Maybe he saw it on our luggage in the car," Joe reasoned. "You think he's in cahoots with the blond girl who drives the Alfa Romeo?"

"Possibly. Or he may have something to do with the mysterious disappearance of the paintings."

Suddenly, Frank changed the subject and started to talk about the delicious food and the picturesque town of Glocken. Joe, assuming his brother did this on purpose, looked around casually. He noticed an elderly gentleman at the table next to theirs—he had been there the night before.

After the boys left the dining room, Frank said, "Did you see the guy at the next table? He listened to every word we were saying. When I mentioned the paintings, he literally pricked up his ears!"

"Well, everyone's talking about the paintings," Joe said. "But if he was really listening, he might have picked up something last night when we had dinner with Gerhard. Our names, for instance."

"Right," Frank said unhappily.

Next morning after breakfast, the boys walked to the city hall to see the mayor. "Do you have a clue yet?" Reimann asked them anxiously.

"Not so far," Joe admitted.

"Don't feel bad," Reimann assured him. "The police haven't gotten anywhere, either."

"Could you tell us about the history of the paintings?" Frank asked.

"I'll try," Reimann said. "Unfortunately, I came here just a few years ago and can only repeat what I was told."

He reported that Mayor Altenberg had decided to put the paintings in a safe place after the first air raid by the Allies. "Altenberg confided in three colleagues, and one night they brought the treasure to a secret place. It was not to be recovered until after the war, when there would be no more danger of its being destroyed. Altenberg asked his co-workers not to reveal the hiding place to anyone."

"Who were those people?" Frank inquired.

"One was the deputy mayor, Palm. The second was Councilman Schmidt, and the third one was a man named Blendinger. He was in charge of the museum."

"And all four perished in the war?" Joe asked.

"I'm only sure about Altenberg," Reimann replied. "He was executed by the Gestapo because he wanted to turn the city over to the Americans in 1945."

"How terrible," Joe murmured.

"Schmidt is said to have been killed in combat, and Palm supposedly died of natural causes. That leaves Blendinger, who is rumored to have drowned in the Rhine River. But his corpse was never found, only his clothes."

Reimann paused for a moment, then went on, "Herr Lechner might be able to tell you more. He was here during Altenberg's tenure. He's out today, but tomorrow he should be back to work."

The Hardys thanked the mayor and left the city hall. Immediately, Joe began to talk about Blendinger. "Do you think he stole the paintings and left his clothes at the riverbank so people would think he was dead?"

Frank shrugged. "Let's go see Doris Altenberg. Maybe she can tell us something, and also let us search the wine cellar."

The boys left their car where they had parked it and walked through the narrow streets toward the huge east gate set into the wall around the city. A slightly rising path led from there to the Altenberg house.

A German shepherd barked furiously when they arrived. "Kaiser, shut up!" Doris Altenberg called out as she appeared in the doorway.

"Are you by any chance the Hardy boys?" she asked with a friendly smile. "Herr Reimann told me you had offered to help find the treasure and would probably come to see me. Please come in." She led the boys into a large, airy living room furnished in heavy oak. On the walls hung a collection of spectacular photographs of the surrounding area.

"Did you take these?" Frank inquired.

"Yes," Doris replied. "It's a hobby of mine. I have my own darkroom in the house."

"Have you always lived here?" Joe asked as they all sat down.

"No. I was only five when my father was shot, and my mother died a few days later. I was brought up by my aunt in Lüdenscheidt, but always spent my school vacations here."

"Who took care of this house?" Frank inquired.

"Karl and Lina, our housekeepers. They've managed the place all these years and are like parents to me."

"Would they have noticed it if someone had gone into the cellar?" Frank asked.

"We've asked them that before," Doris replied. "They insisted that they would have."

"Could we talk to them ourselves?" Frank asked.

"Certainly. I'll go find them. Be back in a minute." A few moments later, Doris returned with Karl and Lina.

They were in their seventies, with white hair and friendly faces. After they had been introduced to the boys, Frank asked, "Could someone have sneaked into the cellar without you noticing it?"

"No way," the old man replied. "We never left the house alone in all those years. For a long time, our married daughter lived here with her family, but now they've moved to Düsseldorf."

"How about at night?"

"The dog would have barked."

The boys were disappointed. Apparently, the intruder could not have gotten into the place!

6 Futile Chase

After Karl and Lina had left the room, the boys continued their conversation with Fräulein Altenberg. "I have a nephew in Frankfurt who's studying art," she said. "He wanted to write a paper on the paintings and could hardly wait to see them. He's very disappointed."

"Do you think we could search the cellar?" Frank inquired.

"Of course. But let me settle another matter first. Where are you staying?"

"At the Glockenhof."

"Why don't you come and move in here? I'd love to have the company of young people, and it might facilitate your investigation."

"Oh, that's very nice of you," Frank said, "but we don't want to impose—"

"Nonsense. Go and get your things, then you can do all the sleuthing you want."

Grateful, the boys hurried back to their hotel. They were in the middle of packing their clothes when they heard approaching footsteps that suddenly stopped in front of their door. But no one knocked and the footsteps faded again toward the stairs.

"You think someone was on the wrong floor?" Frank finally asked. He was in the middle of changing his clothes and at this point stood in his underwear. He went to the door and opened it just a crack. No one was in the hallway. Frank was just about to shut the door again, when he saw a note tacked to the outside.

YOU SNOOPING AMERICANS, GO HOME
OR YOU'LL BE DEAD!

With a quick call to Joe, Frank rushed out of the room and ran down the hallway. "I'll get this creep!" he vowed under his breath. Suddenly, he saw a figure clad in underwear running toward him, followed by a tall, slender youth with blond hair. He stopped short and suddenly realized he himself was the fellow in the underwear, running toward a huge mirror next to the stairway. The youth behind him was his brother!

Joe rushed past Frank, yelling, "Dummy!" in his brother's direction and then turned down the stairs. There he met an old man with a bent back who was on his way down, balancing himself with a walking stick. When he heard the boy behind him, he turned and said in a hoarse voice, "Careful, young man! I almost got run over by another guy a couple of seconds ago!"

Joe stopped and caught his breath. "What'd he look like?"

"Red hair and shabby clothes. A bum!" The old man squinted through his eyeglasses. He had a gray beard and a hat pulled low over his forehead. "The fellow raced out of here as if the devil himself were after him," he added.

Joe thanked him, then hurried across the lobby and through the door into the town square. He looked in all directions, ran to the next block, and looked around again. No red-haired man was in sight!

Disappointed, the boy shrugged and returned to the hotel just as the old man came out.

"Didn't find him, eh?" he rasped. "What's going on, anyway? Oh, well, young people today—" He shook his head and shuffled down the street.

Joe went into the lobby and asked the desk clerk

if a red-haired man had left the hotel a short time before.

The clerk shook his head. "No. The only person besides you that I saw in the last five minutes was that old man."

"Is he a guest?"

"No. Never met him before. I had gone to the office for a moment. He must have come in when I wasn't at the desk."

Suddenly, the truth dawned on Joe. The culprit had been the old man! He had put the warning on their door, then made up the story about the red-haired bum to divert attention from himself.

Joe ran out into the square for the second time and tried to spot the man. There was no sign of him anywhere. Grumbling, Joe returned to the hotel and went up to their room. On the way, he met his brother, now fully clothed, looking a bit embarrassed.

Despite his disappointment, Joe had to laugh. "Too bad the mirror was there," he said, "otherwise the good citizens of Glocken would have had the pleasure of watching you chase a crook in your underwear!"

"Go ahead and laugh," Frank said. "Where's the crook?"

Joe shrugged. "I lost him." Quickly, he told his brother what had happened.

"I guess we both blew it," Frank said as they went back to their room.

"That old man wasn't old," Joe added. "Otherwise he couldn't have disappeared so quickly. That getup he wore was a disguise!"

"Well, he did it all for nothing!" Frank declared. "We're not leaving!" He took the note from the door and looked at it closely. The message had been printed on a piece of white cardboard with a red crayon.

Quickly, the boys finished packing and went into the lobby. On the way, they met the elderly man who had listened to their conversation in the dining room the previous two nights. He looked curiously at their luggage.

"You're leaving Glocken already?" he asked.

"No, we're just changing our lodging," Joe replied.

"You're the Hardy boys, aren't you?" the man went on. "My name's Julius Braun."

"How do you know who we are?" Frank asked suspiciously.

"Oh, word gets around. I know you're investigating the case of the missing pictures."

Frank answered evasively, wondering what the man had overheard when he sat at the next table in the dining room.

"You're probably curious why I'm interested in this," Braun went on. "You see, I'm an art dealer and would just love to see the famous paintings while I'm here on vacation."

He asked a few more questions, but the boys did not volunteer anything, and finally the nosy art dealer walked away.

Before Frank and Joe left the hotel, Frank called Gerhard to tell him of their change in lodging. Their friend was worried about the latest developments and advised the boys to be very careful.

"I have some news too," he added. "I checked with various newspapers this morning to see if they had sent a reporter to Alfred Wagner last Friday. One of them, the *Isarpost*, did."

"You mean the blonde really *was* a journalist?" Frank asked.

"Right. I went to talk to her. She's still mad at poor Alfred."

"Then she wasn't that crazy driver on the Autobahn?"

"No. She couldn't have been. The Alfa Romeo doesn't belong to her. She drives a Volkswagen."

"Wait a minute. You're saying that the sports car belongs to another blonde?"

"Yes. She could be acting as a contact between one of Wagner's employees and whoever wants the sub plans. Suppose she happened to be there when you arrived, overheard you talk to Wagner, then followed you all the way to the Autobahn?"

"She must have hidden well in that case," Frank replied. "We didn't see another blonde at the garage. Matter of fact, the reporter was the only girl there!"

"H'm. I'm going to Wagner's right now," Gerhard went on, "and try to find out who owns that red Alfa Romeo. Talk to you later!"

On the way to the Altenberg house, the boys discussed what they had just learned. When they went through the town gate, a red sports car suddenly came out of a side street and moved in front of them.

"Joe, look, an Alfa!" Frank cried out.

"Only the driver isn't a girl," Joe replied. "But he has a Munich number. Let's follow him!"

Just then, they were caught in a minor traffic jam on the other side of the gate, and the boys had no choice but to pull up close to the red sports car. They were worried about being noticed by the driver, who was adjusting his rear mirror, his head slightly turned.

He was a young man, dressed in a white shirt under a green pullover. On his head he wore a jaunty green cap. His face was dark-complexioned, and his small mustache made him look like a Spaniard.

"Frank!" Joe whispered excitedly. "I think that's the guy who sneaked up to our car the other night!"

Just then, traffic loosened up and the car in front began to move. Frank followed. Instead of turning into the lane that lead to the Altenberg house, they drove down a street paralleling the Rhine River.

The young man drove slowly, forcing Frank and Joe to keep a safe distance.

"How long is he going to creep along like this?" Joe muttered impatiently when the red car leisurely headed into a curve. Two more curves followed right afterward, and by the time the boys came out of the last one, the street ahead of them was empty!

7 A Horrible Discovery

"Step on the gas, Joe!" Frank cried out. "He's not going to get away that easily!"

The Porsche shot forward. But less than three miles ahead, they found themselves in a small town, and wound up behind a large truck that trundled along at a snail's pace. It took a while before Joe could pass it and resume his chase.

"If this keeps up, we'll never catch the crook!" he muttered angrily as he stepped on the gas again. But after a few miles, they both had to admit that their chase was futile, and that the red sports car had vanished without a trace.

"I'm sure that guy drove slowly on purpose," Frank declared. "He knew the road and figured that in that series of curves he could get rid of us!"

"I bet it's the same car we encountered on the Autobahn. Only this time it had another driver."

"For all we know, the driver was the person who put the warning sign on our door, disguised as the old man," Frank said. "Apparently he wants to get rid of us. One way or another!"

"One thing I can't figure out," Joe said, "is why they followed us to Glocken. As long as we're not in Munich, they have nothing to worry about!"

Frank nodded. "Well, at least we know now who's after us. A Spanish-looking man and a blond woman, who drive the same car."

When the boys arrived at the Altenberg home, Kaiser barked loudly, but less ferociously than before. Apparently, he was getting used to them. Doris Altenberg showed them their room on the second floor. They were impressed with their comfortable accommodations filled with antique furniture. They unpacked their clothes quickly, then Joe plopped down on one of the high brass beds. He almost drowned in the fluffy feather comforter.

"Boy, I love these," he declared. "It's like sleeping on a cloud. Don't wake me up early tomorrow, okay?"

"We've got work to do, Joe," Frank said. "And if you don't rise voluntarily, I'll use that jug of water over there!"

"Sadist!"

"Come on now, it isn't nighttime yet. Let's search the cellar," Frank urged.

The police had found no clues in the secret room, but had deduced that the theft must have taken place a long time ago because of the dust and cobwebs on the old chest.

Frank and Joe got powerful flashlights from their car and climbed down the dimly lit staircase. The secret door was unlocked, and they entered the hiding place.

"Spooky, isn't it?" Joe said. "Like a tomb!"

The beams of their flashlights moved over the heavy chest to the caved-in back wall.

"Let's start over there," Frank suggested.

Carefully, they poked around the debris and searched among the rocks and crumbling stones.

"Apparently, the cellar once reached pretty far into the hill," Joe said. "You can't even determine where it ended anymore."

Finding nothing in the pile of rocks, they examined the walls and floor, hoping one of the cinderblocks might be loose and hide a secret. But they had no success. Suddenly, they heard a scratching sound near the door. They turned their lights in that direction and stared into a pair of glowing eyes!

Joe was so surprised he dropped his flashlight. "W-what—" he muttered.

Frank, who had recognized the eyes, chuckled. "Here comes the ghost of the Sexton!" he intoned in a deep voice. But then he clicked his tongue. "Kaiser, what are you doing here? Come over here!"

The German shepherd hesitated, wagged his tail, then finally moved close enough for Frank to pet him.

"That critter scared me to death!" Joe complained and picked up his flashlight.

Kaiser walked around the cellar and sniffed here and there. When he reached a pile of debris, he suddenly whined and began to dig.

The boys watched him with curiosity. "What's there, Kaiser?" Frank asked. "Are you looking for a bone?"

The dog paid no attention. Instead, he continued digging furiously with his front paws.

"Maybe he's on to something," Frank said. "I'll get a shovel!" He ran off, while Joe tried to calm the excited animal. Soon Frank returned with a spade and dug into the pile of stone. After a while, he stopped, wiping perspiration from his forehead.

"Nothing there," he declared. "That dog's crazy."

But Kaiser continued to whine and kept scratching in the debris. Frank resumed digging with his spade while Joe held the flashlight. Suddenly, something white came into sight.

59

"What on earth is that?" Joe asked. "It really looks like a bone!"

Frank put aside the spade, and the boys dug with their hands. "That's not only one bone," he declared, "that's a whole lot of them—pelvis, thigh—" His voice trailed off as the Hardys stared at each other in horror.

"It's—it's a human skeleton!" Joe whispered finally. "I told you, it felt like a tomb in here!"

Taking Kaiser along, the young detectives hurried out of the cellar and into the house, where they told Doris Altenberg about their find.

She instantly called the mayor and reported what happened.

"Too bad we don't know when the cellar caved in," Reimann said. "It could have been hundreds of years ago! Well, I'll phone the police right away, and we'll be out there as soon as possible."

Fifteen minutes later, the mayor arrived with two uniformed officers. They excavated the skeleton and took photographs.

"We'll have to send all this to Frankfurt for further evaluation," the mayor declared.

A clue had been uncovered in the shape of a wedding ring on one of the skeleton's fingers. It bore the name "Bertha" and the date 19·5·40.

"Let's check the records and see who got married that day," Frank suggested.

Reimann promised to take care of it. "The medical examination of the skeleton might also help to identify the victim," he said.

"Do you think he was murdered?" Frank asked.

"Either that, or he was killed when the wall crumbled. His skull is crushed."

After Reimann and the two officers left, Frank and Joe tried to find an answer to the riddle. But after a while they gave up. They were just crossing the yard to the house when Joe spotted a round figure walking along the street.

"Look who's coming," he said. "Our nosy friend, the art collector."

"Lovely place!" Braun called out when he noticed the boys, and described in detail the walk he had just taken. When he stretched out his left hand to indicate the way, the brothers suddenly made a startling discovery. Part of his left ring-finger was missing! Julius Braun was the man who had asked the Frankfurt coin dealer about gold *Joachimstaler*!

8 *Two Hunches*

"Oh, excuse me, Herr Braun," Joe said with a wink at his brother. "I forgot something."

He ran into the house and up the stairs to their room. Quickly, he got his camera from a drawer, put the telephoto lens in, and went to the window. He was hoping that Frank would still be talking to the art dealer.

As he looked out, he saw the two engrossed in conversation, but Braun's back was turned to the window! Cautiously, Joe tried to get Frank's attention by moving the drapes. When Frank finally glanced up, he put a finger to his lips and held up the camera.

Frank got the message. Slowly, he began to shift

his position. Without being aware of it, the art dealer followed suit. Finally, Joe was able to take a half dozen pictures from the window. When he was finished, he whistled contentedly and went downstairs again.

As Joe approached, Braun was just saying goodbye to Frank. Once he was gone, both boys laughed gleefully.

"That was a great idea!" Frank complimented his brother. "Although it wasn't easy for me to push that guy around into the right position!"

"I bet Braun's the man who visited Herr Rehm," Joe said. "And I don't believe he's here on vacation. Probably has something to do with the missing treasure."

"But why would he go to Frankfurt to inquire about gold *Joachimstaler*? Do you believe he got the same anonymous tip as Gerhard?"

"*He* could be the anonymous caller!" Joe pointed out. "But that doesn't make much sense. Why would he tip us off about the theft?"

"I have no idea."

"Well, I have all the things I need to develop the film," Joe said. "Then let's take the prints to Frankfurt to verify that Braun's the man who talked to Herr Rehm."

Doris Altenberg let Joe use a large, walk-in closet she used as a darkroom, while Frank went to the post office. He wanted to talk privately to his friend in Munich.

"Things are happening in Glocken, eh?" Gerhard said, impressed with the boys' new findings. "But what the connections are, I can't see just yet."

"I can't either," Frank admitted. "Did you find out about the red Alfa Romeo?"

"One of Alfred's mechanics, a man named Tarek, remembered working on it," Stolz replied. "A young man, who sounds like your friend with the little mustache, came in for a minor repair. No one had ever seen him before, and he didn't give his name."

Frank was disappointed. "Well, at least we have his license number. Of course, it may be a fake, or the car may be stolen."

"Let me have it anyway," Gerhard said. "I'll try to check it out with the Motor Vehicles Bureau. Now I have a request. Could you drive down to Düsseldorf tomorrow and do a little sleuthing for me? You're a lot closer than I am."

"Sure. What is it?"

"I'd like you to visit a company called Lemberg Werke. Alfred told me they approached him a couple of months ago and wanted to buy his plans for the sub. He declined."

"Oh, I see," Frank said. "And because they didn't

get anywhere, he thinks they may be trying to acquire the plans illegally now."

"It's possible," Gerhard said thoughtfully. "See what you can find out. Meanwhile, I'll look for the spy in Alfred's organization."

Joe was busy all evening developing his pictures, which turned out very sharp and clear. His brother, meanwhile, read a brochure Fräulein Altenberg had given them. It was dated before the war and contained pictures and detailed descriptions of the missing paintings. Among them was a wooden triptych Frank liked especially.

Before the boys went to bed, they wrote a letter to Herr Rehm, planning to mail the photographs since they had no time to drive to Frankfurt and deliver them. They posted the letter early next morning, then went to City Hall to see Herr Lechner. They were directed to a stuffy little office, where a thin, elderly man with white hair greeted them and offered them two straight-backed chairs.

"The mayor told me you'd be coming to see me," he began.

"Yes. We'd like some information on Mayor Altenberg," Joe replied. "Also on Herr Blendinger."

"Helmut Altenberg was a fine man," Herr Lechner said. "Everyone liked him a lot. Had a summer home in the Bavarian Alps, in Bad Waldsee. When he wasn't there, he'd let his staff use it. Almost all municipal employees were up there at one time or another."

The boys listened politely to the old man's memories. However, they were most interested in Blendinger, who had disappeared into the river one day. As soon as he had a chance, Joe brought up the subject.

"Well, they never cleared up what happened," Herr Lechner replied. "There was no trace of Blendinger except his clothes. He probably drowned while swimming. Water was pretty cold already, because it was in September. Yes, in September 1944."

"Wasn't it unusual for him to go swimming so late in the year?" Frank asked.

"Not for Blendinger. He was an oddball anyway, especially since his wife died. Lived all by himself, and nobody knew him very well."

"We have a theory," Frank said. "Perhaps he left his clothes on the riverbank to pretend he drowned, but really took off with the paintings."

Lechner pulled on his right earlobe. "H'm. An oddball Blendinger was, but a thief? I doubt it. Yet, as I said, no one really knew him well. But if you're looking for a suspect, I know one. Unfortunately, it's been proven that he's dead."

"Who's that?" Joe asked.

"Wilhelm Schmidt, the councilman. After he was called into the army, Herr Altenberg found out that Schmidt had embezzled quite a bit of money. When the police were about to arrest him, in the summer of '44, the report came that he had been killed in combat. Probably better this way for his wife and his son Heinz, who was only a little boy then."

"Where's Frau Schmidt now?" Frank wanted to know. "I'd like to ask her some questions."

"Can't. She took off for South America after the war with her son. Had relatives there. I have no idea what became of her."

Herr Lechner also told the boys that Palm, the deputy mayor, had died of a heart attack a few months after the paintings were hidden. The boys thanked the elderly man for the information and were about to leave, when Joe suddenly had an idea.

"Excuse me, sir," he said. "I just remembered something else I wanted to ask you. Do you know Frau Blendinger's first name?"

"Of course," the old man said, raising his eyebrows. "Her name was Bertha."

Bertha! The name on the ring of the skeleton they found in the secret wine cellar! Was it possible the dead man was Blendinger?

Quickly, Joe told Herr Lechner why he had asked.

"Well, well," the old man said, shaking his head. "I can't believe all this happened in our quiet little town. Tell you what. I'll check the records right now and see if I can find Blendinger's wedding date."

While Lechner looked in the files, Frank and Joe talked to each other in low tones. If the dead man was really Blendinger, why were his clothes found on the riverbank? There was only one explanation for this—*murder*! After the murderer had killed Blendinger, he put the man's clothes on the grass, buried the corpse in the pile of debris in the cellar, and disappeared. But how could he have gotten into the cellar without anyone noticing him?

"The dead man could also be someone else," Joe spoke up. "Maybe Blendinger was the murderer and thief, and left his own ring on the victim's finger!"

Frank looked at his brother admiringly. "Not a bad deduction!"

Finally, Lechner returned. "Congratulations," he said. "The date is correct. You were right, it must be Blendinger's wedding ring."

Frank asked Herr Lechner to tell Mayor Reimann about their discovery, then the boys thanked the old man and left. When they returned to the Altenberg house, Kaiser greeted them with a loud bark.

"Thanks, pal," Frank said and patted the dog. "You helped us a great deal!"

Suddenly, the boy had an idea. He ran into the garden, where he had seen Karl weeding the vegetables. Joe followed.

"Karl, did you always have a dog in the house, even before you got Kaiser?" the young detective asked.

"Oh, yes," the old man replied. "You need a dog in a place like this. I've been here for a long, long time, and we've always had one."

"Are you sure you had one in September 1944?"

Karl frowned. "Let's see—which one did we have in those days? Prinz, that's it. How—how'd you guess, young man? That must have been the time when Prinz was so restless at night and barked all the time. One morning we found him dead— poisoned!"

Joe realized what his brother was getting at and asked tensely, "Did you ever find out who killed the dog?"

"No. Probably someone who was bothered by the noise. The poor animal! Anyway, we didn't get another dog until a few weeks later."

The boys thanked the man and hurried into the kitchen, where they quickly ate a sandwich prepared by Lina. Then they started their trip to Düsseldorf.

"That was quite a brainstorm you had," Joe said admiringly to his brother.

"Well, I realized that the theft could have taken place right after the war. And Kaiser wasn't alive then!"

"Of course not. And the fact that the previous dog was poisoned proves that someone could have gotten into the cellar without Karl and Lina being aware of it. And it all happened at the same time Blendinger drowned!"

"Maybe the thief forced him to reveal the hiding place of the treasure and killed him afterward," Frank said.

With moderate traffic on the Autobahn and a short break for a snack, it was three in the afternoon before they reached the Lemberg Werke. It was a small company, and looked clean and neat.

The Hardys had decided to introduce themselves as reporters for a youth magazine. The receptionist asked them to wait a few moments. Someone would be with them soon to give the information they wanted.

The boys sat down in the lobby. People came and went. A young man in a white lab coat looked at them curiously as he waited for a folder at the receptionist's desk. Finally, a well-dressed man in his forties walked up to them. "What can I do for you?" he asked with a friendly smile.

Joe said they were writing a series of articles for their magazine about mini-submarines. "We'd like to mention the boat your company is developing," he added.

"I'm sorry I can't help you with that," the man said. "We did have a mini-sub division, but we discontinued the development about two months ago."

The boys looked at him in surprise. If the company was out of the mini-sub business, there was no reason for them to steal Wagner's plans. They wondered if the man was telling them the truth.

"What made you give up your project?" Frank asked.

"Internal reasons," the man replied curtly. "I really can't talk to you about it."

The boys tried for a few more minutes but had no luck. Disappointed, they thanked the man and left.

"We're really no wiser than before," Frank muttered as they walked outside and looked around. Just then the man in the white lab coat, whom they had seen in the lobby before, came out the door and walked past them. Without turning his head, he said, "Wait for me at Maria's at five o'clock!"

9 *News at Maria's*

The Hardys were speechless for a moment as they stared after the man. Then Joe made a move to follow him. Frank held his brother back by the arm and pulled him into the street.

"Don't!" he whispered. "Maybe we'll learn something!"

The boys climbed into their car, and Joe shook his head. "I don't get it. How does this guy know who we are? And why didn't he just tell us what was on his mind?"

"He might have overheard us at Lemberg Werke," Frank replied. "Perhaps he knows something about the mini-subs but doesn't want to be seen with us so as not to risk his job."

"Then maybe our trip wasn't in vain after all," Joe agreed. "Let's go to Maria's! I suppose it's a café or a restaurant. Actually, I hope it is. Can you believe I'm hungry again?"

Frank chuckled. "So am I!"

He started the car and drove to the next intersection. Maria's Coffee Shop was on the other side on the left. After parking the car, the boys went inside.

It was a small place with tables on each side of the room. Frank and Joe sat down and ordered hot dogs with potato salad.

Soon the little restaurant filled up with people who had just left work. The Hardys waited with growing impatience for the mysterious young man. He walked in a few minutes past five, said hello to some friends, then sat down at the boys' table.

He introduced himself as Peter Hauser, ordered a cup of coffee, then grinned broadly at the young detectives. "How much is it worth to you to talk to me?"

Frank and Joe stared at each other. They had not expected to pay for the information.

Frank cleared his throat. "I think we'd better tell you what this is all about," he began. "My name's Frank Hardy, and this is my brother Joe. We're working for Gerhard Stolz, the investigative reporter. You might have heard of him."

"I sure have," Hauser said. "Does that mean

you're not really with a youth magazine at all?"

"That's right. We just pretended to be reporters to get some information from Lemberg Werke without arousing suspicion." Frank told the young man the reason for their visit, and Peter Hauser shook his head in surprise.

"And here I thought I could make a few bucks off two rookie reporters. But this is even better. So you're working on a case of industrial espionage? I wouldn't be surprised if this guy Steiner was behind it."

"What do you mean?" Frank asked. "Who's he?"

Peter Hauser explained what had happened to the development of the Lemberg mini-sub. The company had been urged for several years by their South American representative in Buenos Aires to design a small sub that would be able to submerge to a depth of fifteen hundred feet.

"The Argentinian representative, Willy Steiner, felt it was a great idea. Two years ago, we hired half a dozen people to work on the project, among them a friend of Steiner's—a younger man named Heinz Kroll—and myself. We developed different designs, and just as we were ready to build a prototype, the whole thing was called off!"

"So it's true that Lemberg discontinued the sub," Joe said.

"Yes. In spite of all the money that we put into

74

it," Hauser replied. "Later, I learned the reason from Heinz Kroll."

"I think I know what it was," Frank spoke up. "Management heard about Alfred Wagner's mini-sub, which was superior to their own. So they tried to buy Wagner's."

"And when he refused to sell, they just dropped the whole project," Joe added.

Hauser nodded. "Exactly. Willy Steiner was furious. He made a special trip over here, and argued with Herr Lemberg endlessly. Finally, Lemberg kicked him out."

"I don't see why the man we spoke to wouldn't tell us that," Joe declared.

"Maybe he would have if you hadn't claimed to be reporters," Hauser said. "I don't think he wanted the affair written up in the press. In fact, there's something else going on now that even he doesn't know about!"

"What's that?" Frank asked eagerly.

"Willy Steiner decided to continue developing the mini-sub on his own, together with his friend Heinz Kroll and a man named Oskar Jansky. Both were with Lemberg but left. They're building their ship in Munich—I don't know their address, though. Later, they're going to test it in a little Bavarian lake."

"How do you know all this?" Frank asked.

75

"From Heinz Kroll," Hauser replied. "He wanted me to go with them. Initially, I pretended to be interested, just to find out what they were up to. He promised me the world, too. He was really ticked off when I said no."

Hauser ordered another cup of coffee and took a long sip. "I had no intention of working with these people. For one thing, I can't stand Heinz Kroll. He's a slippery character, that one. And Jansky I don't trust, either. Besides, the whole thing looked rather fishy to me. Heinz claims that our company didn't handle Wagner right, but that Steiner didn't have any trouble."

"Sure he didn't," Frank said. "He didn't ask Wagner to sell his plans—he just took them! We'll have to stop those crooks before they get too far. I hope we won't have any trouble finding them in Munich."

Joe asked the young man what the three suspects looked like. Hauser said he had never met Willy Steiner, but Jansky was about six feet tall, skinny, and had gray hair. When he described Heinz Kroll, the Hardys gaped in surprise. There was no doubt that he was the man whom they had seen in the red sports car!

Frank and Joe thanked Peter Hauser, who promised to let them know if he heard anything further from Kroll. Then he shook hands with the Hardys and grinned. "I never thought I'd be helping Gerhard Stolz with one of his investigations!"

The young detectives decided to drive back toward Glocken and call Gerhard from a rest area later because it was too early to catch him home. They stopped near Limburg and went to a telephone booth.

Rita Stolz answered. "Gerhard isn't here," she said. "I have no idea where he is. Said he'd eat out. Shall I leave him a message?"

"Please," Frank said. "Tell him we have some important news for him. We'll try to get in touch with him later."

"Okay. Oh, wait a minute. I just noticed that Gerhard left a note for you on this telephone pad. It says, 'Alfa license number phony.'"

"Thanks, Rita. Good thing it doesn't matter now in view of the new development."

It was late at night when the boys arrived in Glocken. Joe had tried to reach Gerhard once more, but he hadn't returned.

Next morning after breakfast, the boys drove to the post office. Doris Altenberg had offered them her telephone, but they did not want to take advantage of her hospitality. Joe went into a booth and dialed Gerhard's number, but there was no answer.

When Joe walked out, his forehead was creased in

thought. Then he heard a low whistle. He realized that it came from Frank, who stood in the town square waving to him.

"What's up?" Joe asked after he hurried to his brother.

"I just saw Herr Braun come out of the Glockenhof," Frank replied. "See, there he is. Let's follow him for a while. Maybe something interesting will turn up."

Joe agreed. If the art dealer should notice them, they could just walk up to him and start a conversation.

Braun did not seem to be going anywhere in particular. When he came to an intersection, he suddenly stopped and looked intently down into the side street. Frank and Joe glanced into a shop window, watching the little man out of the corners of their eyes. Just then, Braun rushed around the corner in a flash!

10 A Bird Flies Away

"After him!" Joe urged.

But Frank held his impulsive brother back. "Wait a minute. If we run around the corner, he'll realize we're after him. Let's cross the intersection and just look down the side street in a casual manner."

The boys pretended to be deep in conversation as they crossed the street. Frank glanced past Joe and whispered, "He's halfway down the block talking to a guy in a blue car. They're too far away for me to really see much. Now Braun's getting into the car. Drat, they're taking off! Too bad."

Joe turned and saw the car round the next corner, but neither he nor Frank could read the license number. There was no way to follow the art dealer, because their Porsche was parked in the town square.

"Do you think that character in the blue car has something to do with the gold *Joachimstaler* and the paintings?" Joe asked.

"Who knows?" Frank replied. "Maybe he was just a casual acquaintance of Braun's."

"Perhaps we should call Herr Rehm in Frankfurt," Joe suggested. "He must have the photos by now. Perhaps he'll be able to identify Braun."

"Good idea," Frank agreed, and headed for the next phone booth. A few minutes later, he emerged with a smile. Lothar Rehm had confirmed their suspicion: the man with the missing part of his finger was the art dealer! Now the boys were convinced that Braun had some connection with the theft of the paintings, but they still were not sure why he wanted to know who had sold gold *Joachimstaler*.

"Maybe he'll be back at the Glockenhof this afternoon," Joe suggested. "We can pay him a visit and try to find out what he's up to then. Now I suggest we go back to the Altenberg house. Maybe Gerhard called and left a message."

But Gerhard Stolz had not called. Instead, a telegram was waiting for them. Frank opened it and frowned. "Listen to this," he said to his brother and

80

read the message. " 'Clues lead to Vienna stop will go there for a few days stop Gerhard Stolz.' "

"Vienna?" Joe asked. "That's strange. Do you think Steiner and his gang took off for Austria?"

Frank shrugged. "Too bad we can't contact him. We have so much to tell him!"

"I can't figure out why he sent a telegram instead of calling us," Joe declared.

"Maybe he didn't want to disturb Miss Altenberg so early in the morning," Frank replied. "The telegram was phoned in at six-thirty."

The boys spent the rest of the morning helping Karl with his work in the yard. After lunch, they drove back into town and went to the Glockenhof, asking to see the art dealer.

"Herr Braun?" the clerk said. "Sorry, but he's gone."

"Gone?" Frank and Joe echoed.

"He checked out about an hour ago. He had planned to stay longer, but apparently something important came up. He left in a hurry."

"Do you know where he went?" Frank inquired.

"No. I don't even know where to send his mail."

"Maybe he'll call you. Then we'd be able to get in touch with him," Joe said. He told the surprised clerk that they needed to talk to the art dealer because he could help clear up a theft. The young man promised to phone them if he heard from Braun.

"So our bird flew away," Frank muttered as they left the hotel. "I bet that stranger in the blue car had something to do with it."

Joe nodded. "Too bad. Well, let's go see Herr Lechner while we're here. Perhaps he and the mayor have some more news on Blendinger."

At City Hall, the elderly official gave them two yellowed photographs of Blendinger and a group shot that included Helmut Altenberg and Wilhelm Schmidt. If Blendinger was still alive, the boys were told, they might be able to recognize him from the pictures of him as a younger man.

The boys thanked him and left his office. They decided to call Gerhard in Munich to find out more about his trip to Vienna.

"While you call," Joe said to his brother, "I'm going to have some ice cream. I'm hungry."

He went to a small café on the square while Frank disappeared into the telephone booth in front of the post office. As Joe was ordering an ice-cream cone at the counter, a customer stood up and passed him on the way to the door. He was elegantly dressed, with dark glasses, a mustache, and shiny black hair.

Just then, the clerk handed Joe his ice cream. He took it absentmindedly, then suddenly jumped off his stool and rushed after the mustached man. "Hey, wait a minute!" Joe called out.

Several passersby turned their heads as the young detective ran out of the café. The stranger, meanwhile, kept walking straight ahead. Finally, Joe caught up with him and blocked his way. He pointed to the man's breast pocket that showed part of a blue-and-white-striped silk handkerchief with a sun pattern, exactly like the one he had found near their car the first night in Glocken!

"Excuse me, sir, but where did you get this?" Joe asked.

The man retreated from Joe's pointing finger and stared at him indignantly. Then he tried to pass the boy.

But Joe blocked his way again. Ice cream was dripping down the young detective's fingers, and pedestrians began to crowd around the two, staring curiously. Suddenly, the Italian owner of the café rushed toward them and yelled, *Al ladro! Al ladro!* Joe paid no attention to him. He was too busy trying to find out about the strange handkerchief, while desperately licking his melting ice cream.

The café owner, feeling ignored, became very agitated. He let out a stream of words in Italian that Joe could not understand.

Just then, Frank came out of the telephone booth

and pushed his way through the crowd. When he reached his brother, he stared in surprise. The Italian was gesticulating wildly and pulling on Joe's arm, while the younger Hardy was trying not to get ice cream all over himself and the café owner.

Frank could not help but burst out laughing. Suddenly, a police officer appeared on the scene. The Italian quickly turned to him for assistance, while Joe looked at his brother with a despairing shrug.

"Instead of helping me, you're laughing!" he accused Frank. "Don't you see I'm in trouble?"

"Sorry, but all this is kind of funny," Frank replied. "What happened?"

Quickly, Joe explained the reason for his predicament. Meanwhile, the policeman could not make heads or tails out of the Italian's complaint. He was pleased when Frank turned to the mustached stranger, who apparently spoke no German either, and tried to tell him in English what was going on.

Soon everyone calmed down. The stranger realized that Joe had not meant to attack him, and the café owner was paid for the ice cream. The Hardys found out that the man Joe had followed was from Argentina and that he had bought his handkerchief, the cause of the trouble, in a shop in Buenos Aires.

When the Hardys were finally back in their car, Joe said, "I had a hunch I'd seen that pattern before.

It reminded me of the Argentinian flag, even though that has only one white and one blue stripe with a sun in the middle."

"Right," Frank added. "And now we know why Kroll wanted to retrieve the handkerchief. It pointed to his connection with Argentina."

"Hey, where are you going?" Joe asked suddenly, when he realized that his brother did not turn toward the Altenberg house but continued straight ahead.

"I just had an idea," Frank replied. "Remember, this is the road where Heinz Kroll gave us the slip with his Alfa. We assumed he just stepped on the gas and took off, right?"

"Right. What are you getting at?"

"Well, perhaps he hid somewhere along the way and let us pass. There could be a little alley we missed because we were looking at the street straight ahead!"

"It's possible," Joe agreed. "I'll check the right, you take the left."

Shortly after the curves where the red sports car had disappeared from sight, the boys noticed a turnoff. It was hardly more than a footpath leading into a small valley. Meadows bordered it on both sides, and there was a little vineyard that no one seemed to have tended for years. The boys immediately spotted tire tracks in the dusty road. A car had driven there recently, and both Frank and Joe were sure it was the red Alfa Romeo.

The path turned left, and they saw a wooded hill ahead. Then an old mine came into view. DO NOT ENTER. DANGER! was written on a sign along the road.

Frank parked the car in the shadow of an oak tree, and the boys got out to look around.

"Strange place," Frank muttered.

"You're right," Joe agreed. "There's the entrance, and up there is the foundation of an old building."

"I wonder if Kroll hid here?"

"Let's investigate," Joe suggested and got a couple of flashlights from their car. As they approached the mine entrance, they noticed several more tire tracks on the ground leading inside. The boys went over to the marks and studied them carefully.

"I think these were made by the same car coming and going several times," Frank declared.

"I agree," Joe said. "And I bet it was the red Alfa Romeo!"

Cautiously, the young detectives moved toward the entrance and looked into a large antechamber. They gaped in surprise. Inside, in the semi-darkness, stood the red sports car!

They held their breath and listened, but heard nothing. "I don't think Kroll's in here," Frank whispered finally. "Come on."

They turned on their flashlights and began to examine the elegant little Alfa. Joe opened the trunk with the key he found in the ignition. A collection of license plates was lying inside! Frank, meanwhile, was checking the interior of the car. He discovered an old gray suit and a hat. When he opened the glove compartment, he said excitedly in an undertone, "Joe, look! Here's your camera. And what in the world is that?"

As Joe hastily walked over, Frank pulled out a strange object. Dangling in his hand was a wig with long, blond hair!

11 A Trap!

"A wig!" Frank exclaimed triumphantly. "That explains the blond woman on the Autobahn!"

Joe nodded. "This guy really fooled us, didn't he!" Then he spotted the clothing inside the car. Quickly, he checked the suit pockets and pulled out a pair of glasses and a phony gray beard. On the floor of the car, he saw a walking stick.

"Now I get it!" he exploded. "Heinz not only impersonated the blond woman, he was also the old man who put the warning on our door! Apparently, it had nothing to do with the art theft, after all!"

"There's one thing I don't understand, though," Frank spoke up.

"What's that?"

"What is Heinz Kroll doing in Glocken? And why does he want to get us out of town? He should be happy we're here and not in Munich!"

"True," Joe agreed. "I don't have the answer to that, either."

Suddenly, it dawned on the boys that they had been talking freely with each other. What if someone was eavesdropping? They quickly turned off their flashlights and stood still to listen. After a minute of dead silence, Joe said, "I don't think anyone's around. What are we going to do next?"

"I'd like to check out this mine," Frank replied. "Perhaps we'll find some more clues."

"Or Kroll himself. But we'd better be careful."

Their eyes had become used to the semidarkness, and the boys saw a narrow tunnel at the end of the antechamber.

Cautiously, they went into the passage. It was just wide enough for them to walk side by side. After a few steps, they had to use their flashlights. The tunnel went straight ahead for about twenty yards, rising slightly, until it curved to the left. At the corner, the boys switched off their lights and listened tensely. There was no sound anywhere. They put their flashlights on again and continued.

Now the passage became narrower, and large boulders dotted the floor here and there.

"I hope we don't get hit on the head by one of these," Frank whispered.

They came to a cross tunnel and listened again. There was no sound. The air had become noticeably cooler and more humid, and a moldy smell pervaded the area. Suddenly, they heard a loud rustling! The noise stopped as abruptly as it had begun, and the Hardys were petrified. Was something or someone lurking ahead of them?

They stood stock-still for a while, but finally Joe turned on his flashlight again and walked closer to the cross tunnel. Just then, a shadow shot out of the dark, rushed past them, and disappeared through the entrance.

"Wow!" Frank muttered and wiped cold perspiration from his forehead. "A huge rat! I almost had heart failure because of that thing!"

When the boys had recovered from their scare, they beamed their lights into the short cross tunnel. Joe touched one of the huge, wooden supports.

"They must be ages old," he said. "I wonder how strong they are at this point." He pushed the beam with his hand, and little stones rained down on them from the ceiling. Instantly, the two jumped out into the main passage.

"Are you tired of living?" Frank hissed. "Let's not tempt fate, eh?"

Joe grinned sheepishly, and the two continued their investigation. The ground beneath them rose and fell, and after a few more bends they came to a cross tunnel that had no visible ends.

They stood a while, listening in the darkness, then Frank suggested, "We'd better go back. Otherwise we'll get lost!"

Joe nodded and was just about to put his light on again when suddenly he stopped short. "Wait a minute," he whispered. "What was that?"

Tensely, the Hardys strained their ears and heard a mumbling up ahead.

"Voices!" Frank said excitedly. "Let's go a little closer!"

The boys held on to each other and tiptoed ahead. Approaching a dim shimmer of light, the Hardys heard the voices of two men. The tunnel turned sharply and the young detectives realized that the men had to be just beyond the bend.

Suddenly, Frank stopped and pulled Joe by the hand. He thought he had heard steps behind them. They listened again, but all was quiet, so they advanced a few more steps.

"—have to go! These young snoopers are beginning to become a real problem!" a man said.

"I warned them, and that's it. If they don't get out of town now, we'll have to take drastic measures."

"I bet that's Heinz Kroll," Frank whispered. "But who's he talking to? Willy Steiner or Oskar Jansky?"

"Let's get them and find out!" Joe whispered back. "They'll be so surprised that we'll have a good chance of overpowering them."

Frank nodded, and with a loud war whoop, the Hardys charged ahead, ready to attack their enemies. Aggressively, they barreled around the bend, but suddenly stopped dead in their tracks. There was no one at the other side of the tunnel!

A flickering storm lantern stood on the floor, lighting up a tape recorder that was slowly unwinding.

"Get back!" Joe cried out. "It's a trap!"

But it was too late. Suddenly, a tremendous explosion filled the area. Stones and boulders flew through the air as the tunnel behind them collapsed. Both boys were thrown to the ground and passed out momentarily.

Then there was nothing but black stillness. After a while, Joe moved and coughed. "Frank, are you okay?" he called out fearfully. "Are you hurt, Frank?"

"I think I'm still in one piece," Frank croaked. "But my ears are ringing like a million bells!"

Joe got up and switched on his flashlight. He was lucky it hadn't been damaged. Through a slowly settling cloud of dust he saw his brother, who sat on the ground shaking his head. Then he got back on his feet, knees trembling from the frightening experience.

Joe beamed his light in the direction from where they had come. There was nothing but a mass of rocks, boulders, dirt, and crushed supports. The tunnel was completely cut off!

"We're trapped!" Frank exclaimed, his face white as a sheet. "We'll never get out of here again!"

"We could try digging," Joe suggested lamely.

The boys put their lights on the ground and started to move the debris with their hands. Soon they were perspiring and gasping from the effort. A huge boulder was lying in their way, and was impossible to move.

"This won't work," Joe said. "The cave-in might be ten or twenty yards long!"

Frank leaned on the wall, exhausted. "That means we'll have to find another exit."

"If there is one," Joe muttered. He picked up the storm lantern, which had fallen over, and lighted it with a match. "This way we can preserve our flashlights," he declared.

Tensely, the boys walked forward. They passed

another cross tunnel, but soon reached the end of the main passageway. There was a wall of debris where the tunnel had apparently caved in long ago.

"I feel like a trapped animal!" Frank sighed. "We can't give up, though. Let's examine the cross tunnel."

The boys hurried back, fighting a feeling of panic. The first cross tunnel ended soon, but the second one was a narrow, low passageway that led down into a cavelike room. From there, three more tunnels branched off in different directions. With newfound hope, the boys investigated them, but all three came to an end after a few yards.

Discouraged, the young detectives returned to the cave and sat down on a large boulder.

"We should've known there wouldn't be another exit," Joe wailed. "Kroll set the trap at the right spot!"

"And we were stupid enough to walk right into it," Frank added. "This creep must know the old mine like the back of his hand. I wonder how come?"

"We'll never know the answer," Joe's voice trailed off. He was overcome with the feeling that their situation was hopeless, and that they were buried alive.

Frank, too, was overwhelmed with his own helplessness. "We won't be discovered missing until tomorrow. And then, who would think of looking for us in this abandoned mine? Even if someone had the idea, it could take days for a rescue team to get to this spot! By that time, we will have died from dehydration or lack of air!"

12 A Surprising Development

Joe pointed to the lantern that stood on the ground. "We'd better put it out. We'll need the oxygen."

Frank nodded. Suddenly, he stared at the light and rubbed his eyes. "Hey, Joe! Maybe I'm dreaming, but I think the flame's flickering a little. You know what that means? A draft! There must be an opening somewhere!"

Joe slapped his brother on the back and jumped up. "You're brilliant, Frank! How come I didn't see that? Now I can even feel the draft!"

With renewed hope, the two prisoners searched for the opening. Soon they discovered a crack in the ceiling of the cave, but it was high up and so narrow that no one could possibly squeeze through it.

Joe sighed in despair and slumped back onto the stone, while Frank's mind worked rapidly.

"Cheer up, little brother!" he cried suddenly. "There has to be another opening somewhere. Otherwise there wouldn't be a draft!"

This brought Joe to his feet again, and the two carried the flickering lamp through the narrow passageway into the main tunnel.

"Up there, under the ceiling somewhere, must be the other hole," Frank declared and directed the beam over the pile of debris. "I can't see where else it would be."

"So let's dig," Joe said.

Quickly, they started their task, which was extremely difficult without tools. The boys worked in shifts, since there was not enough room for both of them. After one had been digging for ten minutes or so, he stopped for a rest and the other took over.

Slowly, they progressed until Frank loosened an especially heavy boulder and moved it aside. There was nothing behind it. His hand reached out into empty space!

"We've broken through!" he cried out. Then he added cautiously, "But we're not outside yet. I think this is another passageway."

Their flashlight batteries were weak and the light beams rather thin at this point, so they could not really tell where they were after they had slipped through the hole and worked their way down the pile of debris on the other side. Frank lighted the lantern again and held it up. Suddenly, both boys cried out in surprise. They were standing in a low-ceilinged room with a huge wooden chest in the middle!

"I don't believe it!" Joe exclaimed. "We're in Fräulein Altenberg's secret wine cellar!"

"At least we're safe," Frank said, and sighed in relief.

They went into the other cellar, flew up the stairs, and were about to rush out into the yard when they found the door locked.

"That's all we need," Frank grumbled, and banged his fists against the wood. Instantly, Kaiser began to bark. It seemed like an eternity until footsteps were heard and a man's voice said, "Who's there?"

"Frank and Joe! Please let us out!" Frank yelled.

The door was unlocked and the boys saw Doris Altenberg and Karl standing in the yard. Lina came running up, and the dog jumped around the boys in excitement.

"You look like you've been rolling in dirt!" Lina cried out. "What on earth were you doing down in the cellar? Did someone lock you in?"

"We were worried about you," Doris added. "It's rather late—"

But Frank and Joe suddenly felt too exhausted to explain. They pleaded for a shower and a night's sleep, and promised a detailed report of their adventure in the morning.

The following day their hosts were amazed to hear where the boys had been.

"The mine?" Karl asked, his eyes growing wide. "I never knew you could get into the cellar that way. And who would have ever thought of looking for you there?"

"What kind of mine is it?" Frank asked. "No one mentioned it to us before."

"It's been abandoned since World War I," Karl replied. "At that time, iron ore was mined there, but after a terrible accident it was closed down. Since then, no one ever goes near it."

"It seems irresponsible to have just a little warning sign by the road," Frank said. "We'll have to tell Mayor Reimann about it."

"Yes, you do that," the old man agreed. "I know the entrance used to be boarded up, but apparently the panels have rotted away."

"Or the crooks removed them so they could trap us more easily," Frank said.

"Those terrible, terrible men!" Lina cried, her voice trembling. "You'll have to report them to the police at once!"

"We will," Frank promised. "But first we want to see if our car's still at the mine."

"No!" Lina turned to Doris Altenberg. "Doris, don't allow those boys to go near that place again! It's suicidal!"

But Frank and Joe were convinced that their enemies had left the mine by now, thinking the boys were locked in the tunnel forever. Doris agreed with them, and offered to let them use her car.

Right after breakfast, Frank and Joe left.

"Now we know how the thief got into the cellar to steal the paintings," Joe said on the way.

"Of course," Frank agreed. "The tunnel was probably dug just for that purpose, then the cave-in was engineered in 1944."

"Good thinking, Frank. This would fit into our theory about Blendinger's disappearance."

"What I'd like to know is how come we didn't notice the draft while we were checking out the cellar?"

"There wasn't any. The crack in the ceiling of the cave could have been caused by the explosion!"

Both boys were deep in thought while Joe turned onto the narrow path leading into the valley. "Something I can't get out of my head," Frank finally said. "Heinz Kroll and his partner, whose voice we heard on the tape, must know the mine extremely well in order to trap us like this. Don't you think that's odd?"

"Why? They may have discovered the place accidentally, or heard the local people talk about it."

"But what if it wasn't accidental? What if they've known the mine for a long time, or someone drew them a map?"

"It's possible. What difference does it make?"

"A big one," Frank said excitedly. "If they know the mine so well, they might also know about the tunnel to the secret cellar. In other words, the Kroll gang might have had something to do with the theft of the paintings!"

Joe whistled. "Not a bad deduction. It would explain why Kroll wanted us out of Glocken! But on the other hand—he's involved in the industrial espionage case at Wagner's!"

"Right. Don't ask me how come he features in both mysteries!"

The boys reached their destination and, though they were convinced that their enemies had left, proceeded quietly and carefully. They parked the car some distance from the mine behind a clump of bushes, then slowly crept toward the entrance. Their suspicion proved correct. The Alfa was gone.

Only the silver Porsche still stood under the oak tree.

"Let's see if anything is missing," Frank suggested.

"Missing?" Joe said with a grin. "Quite the contrary!" He pointed to his old camera in the passenger seat. Otherwise, everything seemed to be untouched.

"Very clever," Frank declared. "Now it looks just like an accident. 'Curious kids entered abandoned mine and were trapped by landslide. Rescue discontinued because of excessive danger.'"

Joe chuckled. "Wait till Kroll sees us. Will he ever be surprised!"

"First we'll have to find them," Frank reminded his brother. "I suggest we go to Munich and start searching."

"Good idea," Joe agreed. "There's nothing else for us to do here now anyway."

It was decided that Joe would bring back Fräulein Altenberg's car and start packing, while Frank would call Rita Stolz from the post office.

When Frank spoke to his friend's wife, he was surprised to hear that Gerhard had not been in touch with her. Rita was worried, and so was the Hardy boy.

When he arrived at the Altenberg house, Joe had

packed almost everything. The smell of veal roast permeated the house, and Doris Altenberg invited them to stay for lunch. Gratefully, the boys accepted.

They were all standing in the kitchen when Karl came in.

"Doris, guess who I just saw in town," he said. "Heinz Schmidt!"

Frank stared at him. "Are you talking about the son of the former councilman who was killed in the war?"

"That's right," Karl confirmed. "First I didn't know who he was, because I hadn't seen him since he was a little boy. But afterwards I realized that it had to be Heinz. He looks just like his father. He's driving a sports car. Must be doing well in South America."

Joe almost exploded with excitement. "What kind of car was it?" he urged. "What did it look like?"

"I'm not familiar with the various makes of automobiles, young man," Karl said with a grin. "All I know is it was a little red sports car!"

13 The Man in the Lobby

Frank stared at his brother. "Joe! Did you hear that! Heinz Kroll is probably Heinz Schmidt!"

"I heard. Karl, can you describe Heinz to us?"

After the old man had given them a good idea of what the man looked like, there was no doubt in the boys' minds. Schmidt was indeed Kroll!

"Karl, you've been a great help!" Frank said. "You've given us our best clue yet!"

"Boys," Doris Altenberg interrupted, "would you mind telling me who this mysterious Kroll is? Or would you rather not reveal your findings since I'm still a suspect?"

The young detectives assured her that they never

for a moment believed that she was involved in the thefts.

"We just didn't mention Kroll by name because we didn't realize he had something to do with the paintings," Joe said. "Only as of this morning do we suspect that the two cases we're working on might be connected."

"Two cases?" Doris asked, amazed.

"That's right." Quickly, Joe told her about Alfred Wagner's mini-sub and the reason for their trip to Düsseldorf. He also mentioned the Argentinian handkerchief and the warning they had received at the hotel.

"It all didn't make much sense until now," Frank added. "But since Heinz Kroll is really Heinz Schmidt, the puzzle falls into place. One thing I can't figure out, though. How did he have access to the paintings?"

"Perhaps his father told him where they had been hidden," Fräulein Altenberg surmised.

"That's possible. But Heinz was only a little boy when Wilhelm Schmidt died."

"Maybe Herr Lechner can shed some light on this matter," Joe suggested.

"And let's not forget Blendinger, either," Joe said. "His role in all of this is still a mystery." He sighed. "I can see that we have a lot of work ahead of us."

"You'll figure the whole thing out," Doris said. "You've already discovered a great deal, and I'm sure you'll eventually find the pictures."

"The gang probably sold them a long time ago," Joe said. "I doubt they stole them just to look at them."

"Of course not. But I have a feeling they had trouble finding a buyer," Doris insisted. "There's a good chance that the paintings are still in their possession."

"What makes you think so?" Frank asked.

"Easy. If they had accomplished their goal, they wouldn't try so desperately to get you out of the way. They wouldn't have to, because by now they'd be long gone!"

"Excellent reasoning!" Frank said admiringly. "You're quite a detective, Fräulein Altenberg."

After lunch, the boys thanked their hosts and said good-bye. On the way out of town, they stopped at City Hall to talk to Herr Lechner. He told them that the skeleton they had found in Altenberg's cellar had indeed been identified as Blendinger, and that Frau Schmidt's maiden name was Kroll.

"With his father's reputation, Heinz apparently didn't want to use his name, so he adopted his mother's maiden name," Frank surmised.

Next, the boys called at the mayor's office. Mayor Reimann told them that the town of Glocken, with the help of state authorities, posted a reward of ten thousand marks for the person who found the paintings.

"Wow!" Frank said after they were on their way to Munich. "That's a lot of money. Just think what we could do with that!"

Joe grinned. "We could stay in Germany for another year! Wouldn't that be great?"

After a couple of hours, Frank took the wheel. Joe was glad, since he was getting tenser and tenser the closer they got to Munich. "I just don't understand why Gerhard didn't call," he said. "That's not like him. And this telegram—" He reached into the pocket of his jacket, which he had rolled up and put on the narrow seat behind him. The telegram was not there! Joe turned around and looked in all his pockets, then searched the floor of the car.

"The telegram's gone!" he finally called out. "Did you take it, Frank?"

"Of course not."

"I put it in my pocket yesterday and left the jacket in the car when we went into the mine."

"But we checked everything this morning. Didn't you notice it then?"

"I didn't think of looking for it," Joe admitted. "No doubt Heinz Schmidt took it!"

"Why would he do that?"

"Because it was phony and he didn't want it to be

found!" Joe replied. "I had a funny feeling all along that there was something fishy about that telegram. I'm sure Gerhard didn't send it. One of the Schmidt gang did!"

"That means Gerhard isn't in Vienna after all!" Frank said.

"Right. Who knows? Maybe he walked into a trap and they kidnapped him!"

Frank put his foot on the gas and shot along the Autobahn as fast as he could, since there was no legal limit to restrict his speed. When they came close to Munich, he said, "Why don't we stop at Alfred Wagner's? Maybe he knows what happened."

Joe agreed, and the boys parked in front of their friend's garage. They found Wagner alone in his office, poring over his drawings. The mechanics had gone home some time ago.

"Mr. Wagner, do you know where Gerhard is?" Joe blurted out.

"I thought *you* could tell me," the inventor retorted with a frown on his face. "I was wondering how come I didn't hear from him. I've been trying to get in touch with him since yesterday, but no one answered the phone."

Quickly, the boys told him about the telegram and their suspicion that Gerhard Stolz might have walked into a trap.

"When did you see him last?" Joe inquired.

"Monday," came the reply. Wagner took off his glasses and polished the lenses. "He was here and checked my personnel files. Tuesday morning he called and said he suspected a certain person."

"Who was that?" Frank asked eagerly.

"He didn't tell me, because he wasn't sure. He was planning to trap the guy and find out who his boss was at the same time."

"How was he going to do that?" Joe inquired.

"He made me lock some old drawings in my desk. Then I was to tell everybody in the shop that I'd designed an improved piece of equipment for the sub."

"Oh, I get it," Frank exclaimed. "He wanted to watch the spy when he came in to photograph your papers, and then follow him."

"If only we knew whom he suspected," Joe said with a sigh. "Did anyone work overtime Tuesday night?"

"Possibly," Wagner replied. "I went home at six, because Gerhard had wanted me to. I sent Meier home, too."

Which doesn't mean that he didn't return later, Joe thought. He was still suspicious of Wagner's assistant.

"And yesterday everyone came to work?" Frank inquired. "No one acted suspiciously?"

"Not that I noticed," Wagner said. Unable to give

the boys any further information, he shook his head in frustration. The boys patted him on the back encouragingly, saying they'd keep at it, and quickly left his garage.

It was after seven when they came to a halt in front of the reporter's building. Frank rang the doorbell of their friends' apartment, but no one answered.

"Rita must be out," he declared, "and we don't have a key for the downstairs door!"

"Let's wait until someone either comes out or goes in," Joe suggested.

Soon a woman opened the door for them on her way out. Joe held it while Frank unloaded their luggage and put it into the elevator.

When they were finished with their bags, a tall, muscular man came down the stairs in a hurry. He wore a straw hat and thick glasses, and carried a leather briefcase. When he saw the boys at the elevator, he gave them an angry look, mumbled something unintelligible, and ran out the door.

"I wonder what's bothering him," Joe said as they took the elevator up.

Frank shrugged. "He was probably annoyed that we tied up the elevator and he had to walk down."

When they arrived in front of the Stolz apartment, Frank unlocked the door and both boys went inside. Joe sniffed. "Too bad," he said.

"What?"

"Rita isn't here, and yet I can smell her perfume. She must have just left. I really wanted to talk with her."

Just then, they heard a moan from the living room. They ran inside and gaped. In an armchair was a bound and gagged figure.

Rita Stolz!

14 A Telltale Initial

The boys ran up to Rita and freed her as fast as they could.

"Thanks," she murmured. Frank got a glass of water from the kitchen and gave it to the distraught woman, while Joe massaged her wrists.

"Big man," Rita stammered between gulps of water. "Wore glasses. Left only a few moments ago."

Frank and Joe stared at each other. Both immediately thought of the tall stranger who had run out of the building when they were loading their luggage into the elevator.

"Did he wear a hat and carry a briefcase?" Frank asked.

Rita nodded.

"He couldn't have gone far yet!" Joe declared, and rushed to the telephone. He called the police, where Gerhard Stolz was well known. The sergeant on duty promised to send a squad car at once to look for the fugitive.

"Would you like to lie down?" Frank asked Rita.

"Oh, yes," the woman said, and the boys helped her to the couch, putting a pillow under her head. "I'll feel better in a minute," she added with a little smile. She touched her aching jaw and rubbed her swollen wrists.

"With Gerhard you're never safe," Rita said. "I wish he didn't always have to get involved with criminals."

"How do you know it wasn't just a regular burglar who had no idea that the apartment he broke into belonged to a famous investigative reporter?" Joe asked.

"I know. Why else would he have searched the desk, taken nothing, and then ripped out the top sheets of Gerhard's note pad?"

"In that case, he doesn't sound like an ordinary thief to me, either," Frank admitted. "How'd it all happen?"

"I had just walked in when the stranger jumped me from behind the door. I struggled to get out of his grip, but he shoved a gag in my mouth, then

115

bound my hands and feet with a piece of rope."

"So he was already in the apartment when you came home," Joe said. "Then he must have broken the lock."

"No, he didn't," Rita stated. "He had a key. When he left, he locked up from outside."

Suddenly the truth dawned on Frank. The "burglar" belonged to Schmidt's gang! No doubt they took the key from Gerhard Stolz after they lured him into a trap!

"Now I get it," Joe said at the same time. "He got the key from—"

Frank shoved his elbow into his brother's ribs. He did not want to worry Rita with the news that her husband had fallen into the hands of a gang of ruthless criminals.

Just then the doorbell rang. Two policemen arrived, dragging a struggling man along with them. He was the stranger the boys had seen in the lobby!

"And I'm telling you, you made a mistake!" the man protested loudly. "I'm going to file a complaint against you!"

Rita stared at the trio and held her ears. "What's this all about?" she asked. "I'm still upset after this brutal attack, and I wish you'd come sooner so you could have caught the intruder, and—"

"But Rita!" Frank interrupted. "Isn't *that* the burglar?"

"Of course not. I never saw this man before!"

"See, what'd I tell you?" the stranger cried triumphantly.

Joe apologized to the man for the mixup, but explained that the description of the "burglar" had fit him perfectly, and that he had run out of the building in such a hurry that the boys had suspected him.

"That's because I wanted to catch the train home!" the man shouted. He was still angry and told the group that he had been waiting for fifteen minutes in front of Herr Huber's apartment on the same floor. "I guess Huber forgot we had an appointment," he grumbled. "So I finally decided to leave. Figured I could catch the early train, but the elevator was occupied."

The policemen explained that they had had no trouble finding the man, because he was running along the street.

"I'm really sorry you missed your train," Frank said. "But perhaps you could be of great help to us. Did anyone come out of this apartment while you were waiting?"

"No," the man said, surprised. "But wait—when I got off the elevator, a man was waiting for it. He took it down."

"What's he look like?"

"He was tall and strong, even though he was no

youngster anymore. I think he had a sort of pinched mouth and flat nose. He was wearing glasses, and had on a gray or very light blue suit."

"That's the one!" Rita spoke up.

The police wrote down the description, then thanked the man for his help. He left, somewhat mollified, because the officers assured him that he had been an important witness.

Rita now told the police about the break-in. "The intruder went into my husband's study, searched through the desk, and finally ripped some sheets from the note pad. I could see him through the open door from the living room."

The officers were puzzled. They searched the apartment, found nothing disturbed, and Rita confirmed that there was nothing missing.

"Don't bother looking for fingerprints," she added. "The man wore gloves."

After the officers left, she disappeared into the kitchen to prepare dinner. Frank and Joe, meanwhile, went downstairs to bring their car into the garage.

"Don't you think the intruder was part of the Schmidt gang?" Joe asked his brother.

Frank nodded. "Schmidt probably wanted to know if we passed on any clues to Gerhard, so he sent someone to check the place for evidence."

"The description fits neither Heinz Schmidt nor what we know of Oskar Jansky," Joe reasoned. "So it must have been Willy Steiner."

"Probably. However, the gang might have other members that we don't know about."

"Look," Joe said as they drove into their parking slot in the garage, "Gerhard's Mercedes is gone. I guess that's not surprising."

"I remember he once told us about a good friend of his who's the top detective in the Munich Police Department," Frank said. "His name is Sepp Schirmer. I think we should call him. I bet he can help find Gerhard."

"Good idea. But let's do it from a booth. We'd better not upset Rita."

The boys returned to the lobby where they found a telephone booth. Frank got Schirmer's number out of the telephone book and dialed.

The detective was home and listened carefully to Frank's report. Then he sighed. "I don't like this," he said. "I'm going back to the office after dinner, and I'll send someone to the airport right away to check all the passenger lists. Also, I'll alert my department to be on the lookout for the suspects. What's the license number of Gerhard's car?"

Frank gave it to him, and Schirmer went on. "Perhaps I'll find something in the reports from the last two days. If you hear anything, let me know right away, will you?"

Frank promised to do so and hung up. Then the two boys returned to the apartment. Rita had set the table and dinner was ready. Despite all the excitement, the three pitched heartily into the delicious meal. Later, the boys offered to clean up while Rita rested on the living room couch.

They were drying the dishes in the kitchen when Rita suddenly burst in excitedly. "Look what I found!" she cried out, holding a piece of paper in her hand.

Frank took it and stared at it in surprise.

" 'W. WORRIED ABOUT THE DISAPPEARANCE OF S.,' " he read. " 'CALLED REPEATEDLY. T.' "

"Wow!" Joe exploded. "I bet that's a message from Schmidt's spy!"

"Sure. W. for Wagner, S. for Stolz, and T. is the spy! Maybe Wagner can give us a clue as to what T. stands for."

Frank hugged Rita and kissed her on both cheeks. "You're terrific," he said. "This is a fabulous clue! Where'd you find it?"

"It was lying near the living room couch. Apparently it slipped out of the man's pocket while I was struggling to get away from him." She looked at the boys expectantly. "Are you going to call Wagner?"

"No," Frank said. "I think we should go see him in person."

Frank and Joe rushed out and soon arrived at Wagner's garage. As they had hoped, the inventor was still in his office despite the late hour.

"Do you have an employee whose name starts with T?" Frank asked after a quick greeting.

"T?" Wagner wrinkled his brow. "Yes, I do. One of my mechanics is named Tarek. Why do you ask?"

"Because we think he's the spy for the Schmidt gang!" Frank showed the inventor the slip of paper Rita had found in the Stolz apartment.

"But how can you be sure it's Tarek?" Wagner asked.

"We'll have to set a trap," Frank said. "But first I'd like to find out if the message was written in this office."

Wagner had two typewriters. One of them, an older model, was often used by his staff.

Quickly, the boys compared the typeface. There was no doubt—the message had been written on the older machine!

"Suppose we confront Tarek with the facts," Joe suggested. "He might give himself away."

"No, I have a better idea," Wagner spoke up. "One of you should call the guy and pretend to be Schmidt. Maybe that'll work."

"Great!" Frank agreed. "But why don't we set a trap, so he not only gives himself away, but we can catch him in the process?"

They tried to figure out how to trick the criminal. Finally, it was decided that Frank should call Tarek and tell him to come to the office.

The boy tried to imitate the first voice he had heard on the tape in the mine and said, "S. left a report in W.'s office. We'll have to get rid of it before morning. Please take care of it right away." He hung up before the man had a chance to reply.

Joe laughed. "Now all we have to do is to plan a nice reception for the crook. I can't wait until he gets here."

"Neither can I," Wagner said. He told Joe to hide in a closet in his office, near the light switch, and leave the door slightly ajar. Then he and Frank crouched behind a car in the garage.

Fifteen minutes later, they heard a noise outside. A key turned in the door, and Frank tapped gently on the office window to warn his brother.

Joe clenched his teeth. I can't let him escape! he thought. This man knows where Gerhard is!

Through the window in the office door, he saw the muted beam of a flashlight moving along the floor. The intruder approached the office, opened it, and walked straight to Wagner's desk. He directed his flashlight to the drawers. Joe reached through the closet door and switched on the light. At the same time, he yelled, "Stop! Don't move!"

The intruder whirled around. His flashlight clattered to the floor as his eyes were blinded by the bright glare of the fluorescent ceiling lamps.

15 A Late-Night Row

Alfred Wagner and Frank rushed from their hiding places at the same moment.

"Tarek!" Wagner shouted, grabbing the man by the shoulders and shaking him angrily. "*You* are the crook! *You* photographed my drawings and sold them to Kroll. You might as well admit it, lying won't help you one bit!"

Tarek, a short, stocky man around thirty, was deathly pale. He had not recovered from his initial shock yet.

Frank walked up to him and carefully checked him for weapons. Tarek did not carry any. The boys tied the intruder's hands behind his back and pushed him into the closest chair.

"Where's Gerhard Stolz?" Frank demanded.

"I—I don't know exactly," Tarek stammered. "Somewhere on the other side of the lake in a house."

"You'd better tell us all you know," Joe added, staring at the man coldly.

Tarek said that a few months ago, when he was in a local restaurant, a young man had offered him five hundred marks for "fixing" a stolen car. "Burning off the motor number and painting it a different color, you know," Tarek explained.

"It was an Alfa Romeo and you painted it red, didn't you?" Frank asked.

"Yes," Tarek admitted. "I needed the money, so Heinz Kroll—that was the name of the young man— brought me the car and I worked on it after hours."

"You should be ashamed of yourself to do a thing like that!" Wagner scolded.

"Next day an older man contacted me and put me under pressure," Tarek continued. "Threatened he'd tell the police about it if I didn't get him the drawings for your mini-sub."

"And that was Heinz's partner, Willy Steiner," Frank guessed.

"I don't know. He never told me his name. Anyway, I had no choice but to go along with it. I took a camera the man gave me and had an extra key made to the office. With that, I could come in any time and take the photographs."

"How did you hand over the film?" Joe asked.

"Further down on the lake is a little park. I left my car there when I came here at night to take pictures. On the way home, I left the exposed film in a hollow oak tree."

"And how did your boss know when to look?" Wagner inquired.

"I told him ahead of time," Tarek replied. "I'd go to the park at lunch hour and sit down on a certain bench. If I had a message for him, I stuck it under the bench with chewing gum. He gave me his orders the same way."

"But you made a mistake!" Frank said. "You signed your notes with T., and that's what gave you away."

Tarek started to curse, but Frank did not give him any time to ponder his error. Instead, he wanted to know what happened to Gerhard.

"When Herr Wagner mentioned his new invention on Tuesday," Tarek said, "I decided to photograph it the same night. Everything went fine until I put the film into the hollow oak. Suddenly I heard a rustling in the bushes behind me! I almost had a heart attack, I was so frightened."

"What happened?" Wagner prodded.

"My boss came out of the bushes with another man. Then I saw Herr Stolz lying on the ground, unconscious."

126

"The other man was probably Oskar Jansky," Joe said to his brother. Then he turned to Tarek.

"Why did the two men follow you?"

"When they got my message at noon, they thought it might be a trap. That's how they were able to catch Herr Stolz. They caught him while he was waiting to catch them!"

"What did they do with him?" Frank pressed.

"They carried him to a boat and took off across the lake," Tarek replied. "That's why I think they're holding him somewhere on the other side. It was too dark for me to see which house."

"We'll see if the police buy that story," Frank said.

Alfred Wagner took the cue. "That's right. We'll call the authorities right away. All houses across the lake will have to be searched."

Frank went to the telephone. He contacted headquarters and asked if Detective Schirmer was still there. He was told the officer was on his way home, so he asked the sergeant on duty to have the prisoner picked up and to leave a message for Schirmer to call Wagner.

Now they had no choice but to wait. However, Joe was impatient and worried about his friend, who had been in the hands of the criminals for two days by now. Suddenly, he had an idea.

"I want you to come with me and show me exactly

where the two men went," he said to Tarek.

"And don't think of running away," Frank added. "Don't forget, there are three of us against you."

Tarek glared at him angrily, but offered no resistance as the boys led him through the barn and out to the lakeshore.

The other side of the lake was hardly visible in the darkness. Tarek pointed diagonally across toward a clump of trees. "They stopped near there," he said. "I think there's a house behind those trees. And there's another one to the right, directly on the shore."

Frank turned to Wagner after a whispered conversation with his brother. "May we borrow your rowboat? This way we can find out which house Gerhard is in before the police arrive."

Wagner nodded with some hesitation. "Okay, but be careful, will you?"

The boys promised.

"Wait just a moment," Wagner said. "I want to get my gun from the house so I can keep this bird here under control!" He ran off and returned in a couple of minutes. Pointing the gun at Tarek, he said, "Now move. Back into my office!"

Frank and Joe hurried to the little dock, loosened the boat, then rowed out into the lake.

"Let's not head straight for the house," Frank

advised. "We'd better cross the lake and then advance along the shore."

Once they had reached the other side, they let the boat drift and listened for any telltale sounds. After a while, Frank said. "Come on, we don't have any time to lose."

Silently, they rowed along the shore to the group of trees. The house that stood to the right of them on the shore looked uninhabited.

"Let's try the other one first," Frank suggested.

The boys noticed a small boathouse behind the low-hanging branches of a weeping willow. Cautiously, they approached it. Joe shone his flashlight through the open door and saw a rowboat tied up inside.

The boys fastened their own craft to the dock and climbed out. Joe noticed a long piece of rope trailing on the other boat. Maybe we can use that, he thought to himself, and cut it off.

A narrow, rising path led from the boathouse through the trees. Frank and Joe saw a faint streak of light after a while and realized it came from the house.

"Sh!" Frank warned. "Let's sneak up without any noise!"

As the boys got closer, they heard a murmur of voices. They followed the sound to the window, which was covered by heavy drapes allowing only the small beam of light to escape.

The young detectives pressed closely to the wall underneath the window and listened. A man said something unintelligible, then another replied in a harsh tone, "Five hundred thousand isn't enough!" The boys gaped at each other. It was one of the voices they had heard on the tape!

The first man again said something they could not understand, but he sounded as if he were pleading. Finally came the reply.

"I'm telling you, it isn't enough. I have better offers. And don't forget, a hundred thousand advance at signing of the contract!"

"I bet that's Willy Steiner!" Joe whispered to his brother. "He's probably arguing about the price of the paintings!"

"Or the drawings for the mini-sub," Frank guessed. "Maybe—"

"Sh—" Joe interrupted his brother. The soft-spoken man argued desperately, but the boys could not make out his words. Joe pressed his ear closer to the window, but Frank pulled him back.

"Be careful! Your head was showing above the glass!"

Frustrated, the young detectives waited, not daring to move or breathe. Then the hard voice was heard again. "Okay, you have till tomorrow night to talk to your client. Then I want an answer. Good night. Heinz, will you see our guest out, please?"

"Heinz Schmidt is there, too," Frank murmured.

"Let's go to the front door and check out the visitor!" Joe suggested, and was about to move, when suddenly the yard was bathed in light!

Someone had opened the drapes above them and was staring out into the night!

16 A Violent Fight

Frank and Joe held their breath and did not move a muscle for fear of being discovered.

But then the drapes were drawn again, and the man retreated into the room. Joe let out a lungful of air. "Wow!" he whispered. "That was a close call!"

Quickly, they crept around to the front, where a large yard separated the house from the street. A path bordered by bushes led from the door to the gate at the end of the yard.

The boys were just in time to hide behind a shrub when two men appeared in the doorway. Frank and Joe recognized Heinz Schmidt, but the face of the visitor, who was short and heavyset, was in the shadows. The men shook hands and talked for a moment in low voices.

"I don't think Heinz will accompany the visitor out to the street," Frank whispered. "Why don't we try to catch the little guy?"

"Good idea!"

The boys crept toward the street and stopped behind some dense shrubbery near the gate. They did not have long to wait. Schmidt closed the door behind him after disappearing into the house, and the visitor walked toward them. When he was passing the boys' hiding place, Frank suddenly jumped up and grabbed him in a headlock, which stifled the man's scream.

With a gurgle, he collapsed on the ground as Joe kicked his legs out from under him. He struggled furiously for a while, then lay still. Joe tied his hands and feet, then Frank loosened his grip around the stranger's throat and gagged him with a handkerchief.

"Good work, partner!" He grinned at his brother.

The boys dragged their victim behind the bush and shone a flashlight into his face.

"Hey, Frank!" Joe whispered excitedly. "It's Herr Braun, the art dealer!"

"Some art dealer," Frank grumbled. "Wants to buy stolen property! Maybe it was Steiner he was talking to in the street in Glocken before the two of them took off in the blue car."

"Possibly, but what do we do next?"

The brothers moved out earshot of Braun and debated. "In order to get into the house, we'll have to lure Heinz Schmidt and Steiner outside," Frank declared. It was decided that Frank would wait near the house, while Joe would ring the bell at the gate. When the men came out to see who it was, he would distract them with a cry for help.

While Frank hid, his brother went to the gate and pushed the bell. The door opened and he cried, "Help! Please help me!"

Heinz Schmidt stuck his head out the door and looked into the yard. He heard Joe's cry and stepped out, but stood still after a few yards and listened. Obviously, he did not know what to make of the sudden interruption.

Too bad he's alone, Frank thought; Willy Steiner is still inside. He watched with bated breath as Schmidt advanced a few more steps and stopped only three yards away from him. The young detective made a quick decision. He jumped from his hiding place, grabbed the man by the neck, and pulled him to the ground. Schmidt kicked furiously but Frank, who had the advantage of the surprise attack, kept the upper hand.

"Joe, quick!" he called out.

Joe was already on his way to the house when he heard his brother's cry. He ran up and tied Schmidt in the same manner as Braun.

"I'm glad you brought that rope," Frank said when the job was done, and Joe had shoved his handkerchief into Schmidt's mouth.

Joe nodded. "I had a hunch we might be able to use it. Now we have to get number three!"

The boys carefully approached the house. They walked inside and found themselves in a long, narrow hallway. The floor was covered with an old carpet, and the walls were decorated with rifles and sabers.

Frank was about to close the front door, when the wind blew it shut with a loud bang. The boys froze.

"What's the matter, Heinz?" came the harsh voice from one of the rooms in the back.

Desperately, the boys tried to figure out what to do. Finally, Frank mumbled something unintelligible, while both Hardys went up to the room from which the voice had come. They pressed themselves flat against the door frame.

"What did you say?" the voice came again. Apparently, the man realized that something was wrong. A chair scraped and then heavy footsteps neared the door. The next instant, a tall, strong man appeared in the doorway.

Frank jumped him, twisting Steiner's right arm

backward and shoved his knee into the man's back.

Steiner moaned, then kicked Frank in the shin. Frank loosened his grip in pain and was thrown against the wall by his enemy. Joe smashed into Steiner headfirst and pushed him against the door frame. But the impact was so great that Joe fell down himself.

Quickly, Steiner ripped a gun from the wall and pointed it at the boys.

"Oh, no, you don't!" Joe cried before the man could pull the trigger. He rammed his fist into Steiner's stomach. The rifle clattered to the floor, and the man collapsed with a groan. Both boys pounced on him, carried him into the room, and tied him to a chair.

"That's the guy who attacked Rita," Joe pointed out. "He's the right size and he has the flat nose and pinched mouth the other man described." A pair of horn-rimmed glasses lay on the desk.

Steiner, who had wagged his head in a daze, suddenly stared at the boys with hatred. "It's you? I can't believe you snoopers—"

"You're surprised, aren't you?" Frank asked. "You thought we'd be dead by now."

"Next time I'll make sure you are!" the man hissed.

"There won't be a next time. And now you'd

better answer a few questions, Herr Steiner. Where is Oskar Jansky?"

"Jansky? I wish he were here." Steiner's lips twisted into a sardonic smile. "But today he isn't. Heinz—"

"He's outside, tied up neatly," Frank said. "What did you do with Gerhard Stolz?"

After a small amount of prodding, Steiner admitted that Gerhard was held captive in the basement. A steel door led to it from the hallway.

Frank sighed in relief. "Take his keys, Joe." he said. "We'll search the house later."

"Let's call the police, though," Joe advised, as he fished a key ring from Steiner's jacket pocket.

Frank went to the telephone. He called Wagner's garage first to find out what had happened, and was told by a policeman that everything was under control. Wagner would explain everything later.

Frank quickly reported where he and Joe were and that they had captured the chief crooks.

"Detective Schirmer is on the way here," the policeman said. "As soon as he arrives, we'll get over there."

"Just a few more minutes and the police will be here," Frank announced after he had hung up. Then he and Joe hurried into the hallway.

They found the cellar door, unlocked it, and

turned on the light. Then they rushed down the steps and checked each room in the basement. In the last and tiniest one stood a metal cot. Gerhard Stolz lay on it, his hands and feet bound to the frame!

"Gerhard!" Frank cried hoarsely.

The prisoner turned his head and smiled weakly. The boys cut the ropes that bound the reporter and gently helped him sit up.

"What did these creeps do to you?" Joe exclaimed. "Have you been down here long?"

Gerhard nodded while Frank massaged his wrists. Suddenly, there was a hollow *bang* upstairs. The boys jumped up and looked at each other in alarm. Frank rushed out and raced up the stairs. The metal door to the hallway was closed and locked from the outside!

Angrily, the boy rattled on the doorknob and banged his fists against the panel but in vain. Disgusted, he returned to the others.

"How stupid!" he muttered. "I left the key in the lock. But I still can't figure out who did this. We had these guys tied up safely!"

"Maybe Jansky was in the house after all," Joe surmised.

"You're right. Now we can only hope that the police come soon."

Just then, the boys heard footsteps in the yard,

and a car engine roared to life. Quickly, Joe stepped on the cot and looked out the small cellar window. He saw Heinz Schmidt slam the car door and take off in a cloud of dust.

"There they go!" Joe cried out. "All three of them!"

"Don't worry, boys," Gerhard said softly. "I'm just glad that you two are unhurt."

"Oh, we're okay," Frank said.

"Those men told me you were trapped in a caved-in mine!"

"Well, actually we were," Joe admitted, and started to retell their adventure. After a while, they heard a car drive up and stop in front of the house. A loud thumping told them the door was being forced open. Frank ran upstairs and banged his fists against the metal cellar door while Joe helped Gerhard slowly up the steps. Moments after the captives heard the front door burst open, someone began working on the cellar door.

It finally swung open, and a tall, broad-shouldered man in a baggy suit stood outside, looking dumbfounded.

When he noticed Gerhard Stolz, his face brightened. "Gerhard, I'm glad to see you! And these boys must be Frank and Joe Hardy."

"They are," Gerhard said and introduced the young investigators to Detective Sepp Schirmer.

"Where'd you hide the crooks?" Schirmer wanted to know.

"They got away," Frank replied, crestfallen. He told about the criminals' escape. Unfortunately, he could not give a good description of the men's car.

Schirmer sighed. "Let's hope we can catch them," he said, and ordered one of his officers to report to headquarters. The other men began to search the house.

"I have no idea what the gang will do next," Gerhard said. "They never mentioned a word about their plans."

He gave a quick recounting of his capture, but his friend saw how exhausted he was and how difficult it was for him to speak.

"Tell the details later," Schirmer advised, "when you feel better. Right now I want you to go home and rest!"

Joe supported the motion wholeheartedly. "Rita's worried to death," he said. "I know she can't wait to see you."

At first Stolz did not want to leave, but finally he admitted that he had been knocked unconscious for a while and needed to relax and sleep.

"I'll get someone to drive you," Schirmer said. "He can—"

Just then a policeman came up to the group and stammered, "Boss—I—eh—outside—"

"What's the matter, Hans?" Schirmer inquired.

The man looked embarrassed. "Well, I found this man in the yard. He was tied up and gagged and—"

"Braun!" Frank cried out and slapped his forehead with his palm. "We forgot all about him!"

"Who's he?" Schirmer asked, perplexed.

"He calls himself an art dealer, but we know he's not honest. He was trying to make a deal with Steiner, probably on the stolen paintings."

"He might be able to help us find the gang!" Joe added.

Hans cleared his throat. "No, he can't. He—he disappeared!"

17 Underwater Danger

Four pairs of eyes stared at the hapless man. Then Schirmer thundered, "Would you mind telling me how a man who's gagged and bound can disappear?"

"When he took off, he wasn't bound anymore—I mean, I had untied him," Hans stammered. He explained that he had heard muffled sounds in the bushes and discovered Braun. The art dealer, after being relieved of his gag, had insisted he was a victim of Schmidt's gang.

"Braun's not stupid," Frank said.

"I untied him," Hans went on. "Then he told me there was another prisoner in the backyard. He would show me where. We went there, and while I searched for the man, Braun raced off into the bushes."

"Next time, don't be so trusting," Schirmer grumbled and dismissed the officer. Then he turned to the boys with a sigh. "Now we lost all of them!"

"Maybe not," Joe said suddenly. "Unless Braun has friends in town, he must be staying in a hotel. Suppose we check all the hotels in Munich to see if he's taken a room?"

"Good idea," Detective Schirmer said. "I'll call my assistant at headquarters. We have a list, and he can put a few people on the job. It'll take quite some time to call every hotel in town."

A half hour later, Schirmer's assistant phoned to report that they had located a man who matched Braun's description and who had checked into the Hotel Continental under the name of Herr B. Julius.

"That's our man!" Frank cried out. "Let's go over to the hotel right away and have a little talk with him."

While Joe accompanied Gerhard Stolz home in one of the squad cars, Frank, Schirmer, and two officers rushed to the Hotel Continental near the main railroad station. After the detective identified himself, the night clerk revealed the art dealer's room number. "Herr Julius just got in a few minutes

ago," he volunteered. "He seemed to be in a hurry!"

When Schirmer and his group knocked on Braun's door and were admitted, they saw that the art dealer had been packing his suitcases!

"It seems you're planning to move out in the middle of the night," Schirmer declared. "Well, we'll be happy to put you up at the local prison for a while!"

Braun protested vehemently and turned to Frank. "You know me!" he cried. "Please clear up this misunderstanding!"

"Misunderstanding?" Frank asked. "You might as well admit that you were trying to buy the stolen paintings that belong to the Glocken Museum! We heard you!"

Braun turned ashen.

"And how about Herr Rehm, the coin dealer in Frankfurt?" Frank pressed on. "Why did you ask him about gold *Joachimstaler*?"

Braun mumbled something about police brutality, but did not resist any further. He was taken to headquarters while one of the officers drove Frank to Stolz's apartment.

Gerhard was already sleeping when the boy arrived. Rita had called their family doctor, who had examined the exhausted reporter and insisted that he have plenty of rest.

In the morning, Gerhard felt much better. He had just finished eating a hearty breakfast when the telephone rang. Joe answered. It was Detective Schirmer. Unfortunately, the police had not found a trace of the gang, and Braun was not talking. "But we've discovered Gerhard's car," he reported. "It was parked near the airport."

"Apparently, they wanted to create the impression that Gerhard left it there," Joe commented.

"Right. I'm going to have somebody get the car. Why don't we all meet at Schmidt's place at noon? By that time, we may have picked up another clue."

"Fine. We'll have to get our Porsche at Wagner's house anyway."

Joe wanted to tell Gerhard about his conversation, but Rita stood in front of his bedroom door like a sentry. "Psst!" she warned. "He's sleeping again. Don't disturb him."

"Okay," Joe said. "When he wakes up, tell him we're at Wagner's."

The boys took the subway and a bus to the inventor's house and found Wagner in his office. Frank and Joe immediately told him everything that had been happening. Then, eagerly, they retrieved the Porsche and drove around the lake to Schmidt's place. In the daylight, it looked rather unkempt. Schirmer was already there and told them that the house had been empty for quite a long time before Schmidt and Steiner had rented it.

"It's a great hiding place," the detective said. "The neighbors had no idea what was going on here."

The group went to investigate a wing of the house they had not searched the night before. A connecting door led into it from the hallway. When they saw that the entire area consisted of one large workshop, they gaped. In the middle sat the half-finished body of a mini-sub!

"That's what the gang built from Wagner's drawings!" Frank cried out. "They copied his boat!"

Schirmer nodded. "And all the plans are still here on the drawing board. Apparently, the crooks didn't have enough time to take them along."

The three inspected the boat from all sides. As far as the boys could determine, it was an exact replica of *Ludwig II*. None of them, however, could figure out what the crooks intended to do with it.

"Jansky was probably working here last night when you two arrived on the scene," the detective guessed. He pointed to a bell next to the door. "It's connected with a button underneath Steiner's desk. He must have maneuvered himself toward it along with the chair he was tied to while you were in the cellar."

Frank grimaced. "I suspected something like that. We should have known it was fishy when

Steiner revealed Gerhard's hiding place without much hesitation."

"Do you have any clue regarding the paintings yet?" Joe asked the detective.

Schirmer shook his head. "I found nothing in the house. But I'm having the whole property searched. Also, we're keeping the place under surveillance in case the crooks return."

The boys drove home for lunch. Gerhard was sitting up in bed reading the newspaper. "I'm really feeling great," he said, "but Rita won't let me get up yet."

After eating ham sandwiches, the boys went downstairs and washed Gerhard's Mercedes, which had been delivered by a police officer. Sepp Schirmer came by later in the afternoon, and Gerhard told again in detail how he had been taken prisoner by the gang. His report matched that of Tarek's.

"I was attacked in the park from behind," he said. "When I regained consciousness, I found myself on the cot in the cellar."

"How did you know Tarek was the spy?" Frank asked.

"He was the mechanic who worked on the red Alfa Romeo, but claimed he didn't know the name of the owner. I remembered that when I checked out Alfred's employees. At that point, I also learned

148

that Tarek had recently spent more money than he made."

"The old story," Schirmer said.

Gerhard nodded. "I made some notes about him on my desk pad."

"Too bad Steiner got here before us," Joe put in. "Otherwise we would have found the information."

Next morning, Alfred Wagner called. He had tested *Ludwig II* for the first time, and the little boat had passed its maiden run with flying colors!

Elated, the inventor invited the boys and Gerhard to come along on his next trip. They accepted enthusiastically, even though Rita was anxious.

"Gerhard, you must promise me not to go down in the sub!" she said. "In your condition, that is not a good idea. Suppose something happens—"

"In that little lake?" her husband laughed. "But I promise you anyway."

The three drove to Wagner's, full of excitement. They found him in the barn, with the door to the lake open.

"Hi, everybody," the little man said happily and shook Gerhard's hand. "I'm so glad to see you well again!"

"I'm fine," Stolz told him.

"Rolf Meier is out on the lake," Wagner went on. "See, here he comes." He pointed to a spot on the water where the surface was suddenly broken by the rising sub. Then the bright yellow craft moved toward the dock and stopped in its little slip. Rolf climbed out of the hatch, fastened *Ludwig II* with a rope that Wagner tossed him, then jumped out.

"Everything's just working fine," he reported. "We're ready for our first passengers."

"Okay, boys, all aboard!" Wagner grinned.

Frank and Joe climbed down the hatch and Wagner followed. Then Rolf untied the boat. While he and Gerhard waved, Wagner closed the hatch behind him before taking his place beside the controls. Frank and Joe sat behind him. They could see through the large, rounded pane in front of them.

"Here we go!" the inventor called out. He started the diesel engine and slowly drove out into the lake. When they were about in the middle, he cut the engine and opened several valves to let water into the buoyancy tank.

"We'll have to take on ballast in order to descend," he explained while the boys watched excitedly. Slowly, the water rose above the boat and surrounded them.

Wagner kept his eyes on a small indicator showing the amount of ballast in the tank. Finally, he pushed a button and closed the valves. Then he switched on the electric motor and pushed the steering rod all the way forward. The boat began to descend like an elevator! First they could see through the water around them, but after a few yards it turned dark green in color.

"Now watch!" Wagner said and drove around in circles. He made a figure eight and went up and down. Finally, he switched on the bright headlight, took on additional ballast, and descended to the bottom of the lake.

"Rather dreary down here," Joe said as they skimmed over algae and other vegetation.

Wagner nodded. He pushed a button to activate the pump that would empty the ballast tank so they could rise again. But suddenly the electric motor stopped and the headlight went out. There was nothing but silent darkness around them!

The boys froze for a moment. They did not dare move, afraid to upset the boat's balance. It was a terrible feeling to be caught at the bottom of the lake without power!

Wagner, however, did not panic. He switched on a flashlight. "We'll fix it," he said confidently. "Probably a short circuit somewhere." He played the beam on the main switch, which also served as a circuit breaker. Indeed, the breaker had tripped! Wagner bent down under the dashboard and directed his light on the maze of wires.

"Ah, there's the culprit!" he called out when he

found a loose connection. "Joe, there's a toolbox beneath your seat. Want to hand me a screwdriver and a pair of pliers?"

"Sure." Joe opened the box and gave Wagner the implements. As the inventor started to fix the wire, they suddenly felt a slight impact. They had run aground!

The Hardys stared at each other uneasily, afraid to think of what would happen if Wagner was unable to repair the damage.

But the little man had no such doubts. Calmly, he kept on working, then stood up to switch on the main breaker. The headlight flooded the lake and they could hear the pump humming. The boys sighed with relief.

"We'd better get some fresh air now," Wagner said with a smile and handed Joe the tools. Then he grabbed the steering rod and brought the boat up. It was not long before he had eased *Ludwig II* into its slip and they climbed out.

Gerhard Stolz was worried when he heard about the mishap, but his friend calmed him down.

"No reason to be upset," he said. "We do have a spare battery for a real emergency."

After a short break, Wagner and the boys went on a second trip.

"This time I'll show you the claw," the inventor said when they were hovering just above the lake bottom. "It's a very useful tool, which scientists can use to collect stones or samples of underwater life."

The claw was a mechanical arm with a hook on the end. It was built into the hull of the ship behind a small sliding door and could be operated from the dashboard with a pistol-grip control.

Eagerly, the boys watched through the window as the claw extended, curled up, swayed from side to side, and opened and closed.

"Unfortunately, there isn't much in this puddle that's worth bringing up," Wagner said. "The best you can hope to find is an old shoe or a bunch of rocks." With a grin, he pulled in the claw.

When they were on land again, Gerhard asked Wagner if he would like to accompany them to the Schmidt house. He wanted to show him the half-finished boat.

"Sure, I'm dying to see it," Wagner said. "Come on, we'll take the rowboat over."

Frank and Joe looked disappointed, and the inventor laughed. "Don't you have enough of the sub yet? If you want, you can go down with Rolf again. Maybe he'll teach you how to steer it."

The young mechanic said he would be glad to, and the boys eagerly climbed into the sub again. Meanwhile, Stolz and Wagner rowed toward the house on the other side of the lake. They inspected the workroom, and Wagner was utterly indignant

153

when he saw the copy of his boat. "It's exactly like *Ludwig II*, down to the last detail!" he grumbled.

Later, Detective Schirmer joined them, and they discussed the tangled mystery for a long time. When Gerhard and Alfred finally returned to Wagner's place, it was already dark. There was no light in the garage and no sign of Frank, Joe, or Rolf.

"Do you think they're still in the lake?" Gerhard asked uneasily.

"Let's see if the boat's here," Alfred replied. But the sub was not in its slip! Wagner went into the barn and turned on the light. He noticed a slightly sweet odor. "H'm, I wonder what that is," he said.

Gerhard hurried over to him. "Chloroform!" he cried out, his face tense. He rushed through the barn and into the garage to Wagner's office. Three motionless figures were lying on the floor—Frank, Joe, and Rolf Meier!

18 *Hunt for a Truck*

Gerhard Stolz kneeled down and felt for Frank's pulse. "Thank goodness he's alive!" he exclaimed.

Just then, the boy began to move, and seconds later the others regained consciousness also, sitting up and blinking their eyes.

"Wh-what happened?" Frank stammered and looked around.

"That's what I'd like to hear from you," Gerhard replied. "But you'd better take it easy until you completely recover from that dose of chloroform you got."

Frank grimaced. "Oh, I remember now. We were attacked after we came back from our trip. First Joe got it when he entered the barn to turn on the light, then myself when I went looking for him. Apparently after that, it was Rolf's turn."

"Did anyone see the attacker?" Gerhard asked.

"I did," Joe replied. "It was Heinz Schmidt!"

"Why can't these criminals leave us alone!" Wagner wailed desperately. "Now they even sank my sub!"

"No, they didn't," Gerhard replied. "I'll bet they stole it!"

He called the police while Frank and Joe looked around for clues. Wagner found that the winch had been used to pull the boat out of its slip. "They probably trucked it away," he concluded.

Frank and Joe discovered tire tracks in the lawn. "Must have been a huge truck," Frank declared. "The driver had to run over the grass to turn the corner."

Shortly, Detective Schirmer and his officers arrived. He ordered the men to photograph the tracks. "But it won't help much," he grumbled. "What we really need is a description of the truck." He radioed headquarters and asked that every patrol car be alerted to look for a large truck with a boat on it.

"What I'd like to know," Frank said, "is why did the crooks want Alfred's sub in the first place? They must have a special reason."

No one had the answer, and finally the boys and

Gerhard said good night to Wagner and the officers and drove home.

On the way, Frank said, "You know, I just had an idea. Maybe the Glocken paintings are hidden in some lake, and the gang wants *Ludwig II* to retrieve them!"

"I thought of that," Gerhard said. "But it probably would be just as easy for a few men to go down in divers' outfits. They wouldn't need a sub for that."

"That's true," Frank admitted. "I just mentioned it because Schmidt and Braun were negotiating about the paintings."

"We don't know whether they were really talking about the pictures," Joe put in. "Braun claims to be an art dealer, but perhaps he really isn't, and they were discussing the boat plans instead."

When they arrived at the apartment, Rita stood in the open door. "I don't believe it!" she scolded. "Gerhard, yesterday you were ill in bed, and today you're already out again until all hours of the night chasing crooks!"

Gerhard hugged her and grinned. "Don't worry," he said. "I feel just fine. A little hungry, perhaps—"

"Well, come on in. I have dinner waiting." Rita led the three to the dining room table. While they were eating a delicious roast she had prepared, they told her about their adventures at the lake.

Suddenly, the phone rang. It was Detective Schirmer. "A company by the name of Bally Transport just reported one of their trucks missing," he said. "It's dark blue with white lettering and has a trailer."

"The crooks may have dumped the trailer somewhere," Gerhard guessed.

"That's what I think," Schirmer agreed. "I'll call you in the morning if I hear any more."

Next day after breakfast, he had further news. "We found the trailer in a rest area along the Autobahn," he said. "But what's more, the driver showed up, near Rosenheim. I couldn't quite figure out his story, so he's on his way here. Want to come over with the boys around twelve? Maybe we'll get something out of the man."

Gerhard and the Hardys arrived at Schirmer's office at noon, eager to talk to the driver. He was a tall, gray-haired man with a pale face and a day's growth of beard.

Detective Schirmer smiled at the three. "Herr Bauer here was on his way to Ulm yesterday to pick up a load," he filled them in. "When he stopped at a rest area, he was approached by two men, apparently Jansky and Schmidt, according to his description. They started to talk to him, and suddenly, one of them shoved a chloroform-soaked rag in his face."

158

The driver took up the story. "When I came to, I was lying behind the cab, gagged and bound. It seemed as if a heavy piece of machinery was being loaded. Then one of the men started the truck."

"Did they say anything about where they were going?" Frank asked.

"No. And they pulled a sack over my head so I couldn't see. They drove for a long time, then went along a bumpy path before halting again. At this point they dragged me out of the truck and carried me into the woods, where they left me."

"How did you manage to get away?" Joe inquired.

"I finally loosened my ties," Bauer said and showed them his bruised wrists. "Then I wandered for hours until I found a small village near Rosenheim."

"Could you show us on a map where your attackers left you?" Schirmer asked.

Bauer nodded and indicated the general area.

"I'll send some men down there right away to question people," Schirmer decided. "Perhaps the truck stopped at a local gas station, or the men ate in a restaurant."

Gerhard and the boys returned home. After lunch, they pored over a map in Gerhard's study. "I wonder why the gang dropped the driver where they did," Gerhard said.

"Well, they couldn't get rid of him before they

picked up the boat because that wouldn't have given them enough of a lead," Frank guessed. "If he was found too soon, the police would have been too close behind."

"Right. On the other hand, they wouldn't want to leave him too near their destination, either," Joe added. "It seems to me they'd drop him off somewhere along the way."

"You mean, their goal is north or northeast of Rosenheim?" Gerhard asked.

Frank held up a hand. "I doubt it. It was probably a trick to lure us into the wrong direction!"

"I bet you're right!" Joe cried out.

Gerhard bent over the map again. "They can't cross the border, so they must have driven into the Bavarian Alps," he finally said.

Frank snapped his fingers. "The young man in Düsseldorf, Peter Hauser, said Schmidt wanted to test the boat in a little Alpine lake!"

Joe nodded. "But which one?" His fingers began to trace the various lakes. Suddenly, he stopped. "The Waldsee, that's it! The Altenbergs have a summer house in Bad Waldsee!"

He told Gerhard that this house had often been visited by the municipal employees of the town. "Probably the Schmidts were there, too! Heinz may have known the lake ever since he was a child!"

160

"Why don't you call Doris Altenberg and ask her?" Gerhard suggested.

The boy did, and she confirmed the fact that the Schmidt family had often stayed in Bad Waldsee.

"Would you like to use our house when you go there?" she asked. "If so, I'll call the neighbors. They have the key."

"That would be great," Joe said. "Thanks a million!"

It was decided that Frank and Joe should leave right away and start looking for clues in Bad Waldsee. Gerhard, who had some urgent business to take care of, would follow in a day or two.

Half an hour later, the Hardys were on their way. It was dusk by the time they reached Bad Waldsee. The Altenberg house was at the edge of the resort, directly on the lakefront. They got the key from the neighbors and made themselves at home in the simple but attractively furnished chalet.

Next morning, Frank suggested taking the rowboat out that was docked at the boathouse to investigate the lake. "I brought Gerhard's binoculars," he said.

Joe nodded. "And to look authentic, we'll take a fishing rod from the boathouse and throw a line once in a while."

The young detectives rowed around the lake for

four hours without finding the slightest clue to the gang. Finally, Joe became hungry. "I could eat all the trout we *didn't* pull in this morning," he declared.

The boys returned to the house, tied up the boat, then went to an old restaurant where they had *Bratwurst* and potato salad. After lunch, they visited the police to inquire about the truck and the criminals. However, there was no news.

"Maybe the crooks needed gas or went food shopping," Frank said when they were out in the town square again. "Let's check out all service stations and groceries."

"Okay. Why don't you take the northern part of the town while I take the southern," Joe agreed. "We'll meet again in an hour."

In the end, even this effort proved fruitless. No one remembered seeing the men or a dark blue truck with white lettering.

"Now what?" Joe asked.

"Let's go around the lake and question people in other places," Frank advised. "Maybe the gang avoided Bad Waldsee on purpose."

For the next few hours, the young detectives continued their search in gas stations, restaurants, and food markets. They learned nothing.

They worked their way about three quarters around the lake, and drove through a stretch of woods. They could not see the water until the street wound down again to a romantic little inlet. A small restaurant with a few wooden tables on a veranda was right next to the shore.

"Let's take a break!" Joe exclaimed. "This looks so inviting."

"You're right," Frank agreed and parked the car.

When they sat down, an elderly man, in leather shorts called *Lederhosen,* approached them. Apparently, he was the innkeeper himself. *"Guten Tag,"* he said with a friendly nod of his head. *"Was darfs denn sein?"*

The boys ordered apple cider, and the man brought them two large glasses. Lingering by their table, he asked what brought them to the town, explaining his family had lived there for generations.

Joe told him they were chasing three thieves and described the men and the truck. The innkeeper shook his head. He had not seen them.

Frank sighed. "If they're here, they probably came in at night, so nobody would notice them," he concluded.

The innkeeper raised his eyebrows. "When did you say these people arrived?"

"Saturday or Sunday," Joe replied.

"Well, I didn't see the truck, but maybe I heard it!" their host declared. "I woke up from the noise at three o'clock in the morning on Sunday! The truck went right up to Bear Lake!"

The man pointed to a small street that wound behind his restaurant and up a steep hill covered with fir trees. "Come to think of it," he added, "it never came back, either. I wonder what it's doing up there?" He creased his forehead.

The boys almost jumped with excitement. They finally had a possible clue to the whereabouts of the gang!

19 *The Secret of Bear Lake*

"What a crazy notion, to drive a truck up that steep, little path," the innkeeper sputtered. "And at night yet! I didn't even realize till now that it hasn't come back yet. Maybe the driver broke his neck!"

"Perhaps he returned another way," Joe suggested.

"There isn't any. At least none a truck could use. You fellows don't know Bear Lake!"

Their host explained that it was a long, still lake farther up in the mountains, about half an hour away. At the end, there was a huge cliff rising out of the water. The rest of the lake was bordered by dense, dark-needled trees. "The lake's incredibly deep and the surrounding woods so dark that no one likes to go there. Especially after the landslide."

"Landslide?" Frank asked. "Was that recently?"

"No, no. It was soon after World War II. A piece of the cliff crashed into the lake."

Frank asked the innkeeper to give them directions to Bear Lake, and the friendly Bavarian went to get a piece of paper and a pencil. Then he drew them a detailed map.

The little street behind his restaurant rose straight up the mountain, where it reached a plateau in the woods and continued until it forked about three hundred yards before the lake.

"The left branch goes to a small clearing on the shore, the right one to a hunting lodge and a boathouse," the man explained.

"Who owns the lodge?" Joe asked.

"The Count of Kranichstein. His grandfather used to hunt bears up there every season. But now Count Leopold only spends a few days a year at the place. Otherwise, hardly anyone goes there."

Joe grabbed his brother's arm. "You see how it all fits? I bet the gang is up there with *Ludwig II.*"

"With whom?" the innkeeper looked puzzled.

The boys quickly explained about the stolen mini-sub, then shook the man's hand. "You've been a great help!" Frank said. Then he looked at his brother. "Maybe we should have some dinner before we leave."

"Good idea," Joe agreed. "I'm starved."

The innkeeper laughed. "Good idea. We can't send you up to Bear Lake on an empty stomach." He hurried into the house to prepare a meal. Joe, meanwhile, went to call Gerhard from a pay phone. When he returned, a platter of smoked ham sat on the table. Then the innkeeper brought a loaf of bread and three fried eggs for each boy.

"Gerhard wasn't home," Joe reported. "Rita will give him the message. I told her where we were going, and that I'd come back here after we locate the crooks. I assured her that we'd call again in a couple of hours or so."

When the boys had finished their meal, they paid their host and climbed into the Porsche. Joe took the wheel. The closer they came to Bear Lake, the more cautiously he drove, trying to listen for any sound around them. At the fork, he turned left and finally switched off the engine. They pushed the car into dense underbrush, then continued on foot to the clearing.

The sun had disappeared behind the mountains, and it was starting to get dark. They could barely make out the hunting lodge between the trees on the other side of the lake.

"You know, it's really kind of spooky up here," Joe said. "Very desolate and somehow depressing. No wonder that—"

Suddenly, Frank held up his hand. Someone had turned on a light in the lodge!

"There they are!" he whispered. "Come on!"

The boys did not want to walk along the street in case the gang had rigged up some kind of alarm system. So they crept through the woods around the lake for almost an hour, using their flashlights sparingly.

Finally, they saw a dim glow of light and realized they had reached their destination. Noiselessly, they moved up to the window from which the light came. The shutters were closed. Joe peered through a crack and saw the back of a man who was sitting at a table. Then he recognized Steiner's harsh voice!

"I don't know, Heinz, but it seems that everything's going wrong," the man complained. "We finally find the thing, and the claw doesn't work!"

"Well, we fixed it," Heinz said soothingly. "Now we shouldn't have any more trouble."

"I hope not. In two hours we should be up again, then we'll sink the sub and take off."

"And Stolz and his two foreign snoopers are out of luck!" Heinz sneered.

Steiner laughed. "As for Jansky—" His voice fell to a whisper, and the boys could not hear the rest of the sentence. Suddenly, Steiner spoke in his regular tone again. "Oh, good, Oskar, there's the chow. Heinz, why don't you turn on the radio?"

The Hardys heard a chair scraping, then the voice of a newscaster. They retreated until they were out of earshot.

"Did you hear that?" Frank whispered. "I bet Steiner is about to do Jansky in once he doesn't need him anymore!"

"We won't let him!" Joe vowed. "We'll have to prevent him from getting 'the thing' from the lake, whatever it is. And we'll have to save *Ludwig II*. But how?"

"We can't call the police," Frank said. "By the time they'd get here, the crooks'll be long gone. So we only have one choice—to hide the boat and call for help later."

"Okay, let's go!"

The boys hurried to the lakeshore. Next to the boathouse, they noticed the stolen truck and a car parked between the trees. Quickly, Joe noted the license numbers.

The moon was shining, and in its light they discovered *Ludwig II* next to a small motorboat on the dock. Set into the hull of the boat was a square instrument with a complicated dial system.

"Could be some kind of echo sounder," Frank suggested. He climbed onto the sub and opened the hatch. Suddenly, he realized that their plan had a weak point.

"Wait a minute," he whispered to Joe, who was about to loosen the ropes. "First we have to put the motorboat out of order!"

"You're right," Joe said, scratching his head. "And the two vehicles, too, so the crooks can't leave before the police come."

"Let's take the rotor out of the distributor of the car to start with," Frank said. He was just about to jump onto the dock when they heard a loud shout. Frantically, Joe called, "Frank, they're coming!"

When Frank looked up, he saw that the door to the lodge was open and someone was approaching them with a flashlight. The boy did not lose a second. He jumped through the hatch, squirmed into the pilot's seat, and switched on the light and the engine.

He heard Joe follow him into the sub and accelerated. The craft moved away just as a man ran screaming and gesticulating onto the dock. Oskar Jansky was only a few feet from the sub!

"Wow, that was a close call," Joe said. He watched as the sub gained speed and moved out into the lake.

Just then, spotlights came on at the dock. "They're going to follow us in the motorboat!" Frank cried out.

"Let's go down," Joe suggested.

Frank cut the engine and let water into the tank while Joe locked the hatch. They had watched Rolf Meier and knew exactly what to do. Before the motorboat reached them, they were out of sight.

"Trouble is," Frank said, "we can't stay down here forever."

"Not forever," Joe admitted. "But perhaps long enough so Gerhard will find us. He'll worry when he doesn't get my call." The boy noticed a map on a hook in the wall and unfolded it. It was a home-made but exact chart of the lake with a dozen crosses on it. Most had black circles around them. Only one was circled in red. Next to each cross was a number.

"That probably indicates the depth," Joe said. "Really incredible, because all are around six or seven hundred feet!"

Both boys now pored over the map and tried to figure out the significance of the crosses. Suddenly, Joe snapped his fingers. "I've got it!" he said. "The 'thing' Steiner mentioned must be made out of metal, because I think the instrument in the motor-boat is a magnetometer! A cross was made for every location where a metallic object was found on the bottom of the lake."

Frank nodded. "Then the gang took the mini-sub and checked those locations. A black circle around the cross means the 'thing' they were looking for wasn't there—"

"And the red circle means they hit pay dirt! I bet it's those paintings in their metal container! But how did they ever end up here?"

"Who knows? Say, Joe, why don't we bring up the box ourselves? I'm sure we're not too far away from the spot!"

"Good idea!"

With the help of the boat's compass, they figured out the direction, then took on more ballast and switched on the headlight. They descended while Joe watched the instruments.

"One hundred meters, one fifty, one eighty—" The boy became tense. "One eighty-five—hold it right here."

Frank stopped the boat as they reached the bottom. They used a large boulder as a point of reference, then began a systematic search. The uneven ground was covered with a layer of black muck. Slowly, they proceeded, now and then seeing a rotted tree trunk or a clump of algae. A few times, they thought they saw the metal container, only to find that it was a large rock when they came closer.

After an hour, Joe changed places with his brother and began to pilot the boat. Minutes later, Frank discovered the box.

"Over there, to the right!" he directed. Both

boys were jubilant. There, half-sunken into the black mud, was a square, metal container with two handles. Were the missing paintings inside?

"I hope the claw works," Joe whispered tensely as Frank manipulated the grip. Slowly, he directed the mechanical arm toward the container, grabbed the box, and carefully retracted the claw. The container came easily out of the mud. Frank locked the claw into position, and the brothers broke into whoops of joy, slapping each other's back and jumping up and down. However, their exalted mood soon diminished when they remembered the quandary they were in.

Joe checked the instruments and became worried. "We only have enough oxygen for another hour," he announced. "Maybe we should go up and look around."

Frank agreed. "If the crooks are still waiting for us, we can always submerge again."

Joe nodded and brought the boat up to a point just below the surface. They had cut all lights, and now strained their eyes to see through the window.

The lake seemed deserted, and there was no light in the lodge.

"The gang skipped!" Frank cried out.

Joe was not so sure. "It could be a trap," he said cautiously. "Let's stay away from the boathouse."

The boys decided to continue underwater to the

clearing, then hide the box and go for help in their car. Using the chart and the compass for directions, they reached the designated area with no problems. The water was deep enough for them to pull right up to the small strip of land. Carefully, they maneuvered the box onto the ground, then jumped out of the sub.

"Don't move or I'll shoot!" a loud voice suddenly commanded. The boys whirled and stared into the blinding beams of two flashlights.

A clicking sound proved the threat had not been an empty one. There was no chance for them to attempt an escape.

Someone stepped up behind them and tied their hands and feet. When they had gotten used to the glare of the lights, they recognized Heinz Schmidt and Oskar Jansky.

"You went straight into our trap," Schmidt sneered. "When we found your car, we knew right away where to expect you!"

The boys heard the motorboat start up at the boathouse and Schmidt went on, "Thanks for bringing up the paintings, by the way. My father will be thrilled to get them back."

"Your father?" Frank was puzzled. "He was killed in the war!"

Schmidt smirked. "He arranged it so everyone believed that. Pretty clever, eh?"

"So Steiner is really Wilhelm Schmidt?" Joe asked.

"That's right," Heinz replied.

"But we saw photographs where he looks completely different!"

"A little plastic surgery can do wonders. Now, no more revelations, even though you two won't have a chance to tell anybody. You're through with snooping once and for all."

He grabbed Joe and, together with Jansky, carried him into the sub. The boy struggled fiercely, but Schmidt's fist landed in his face as he was shoved through the hatch down into the passenger seat. Frank immediately followed.

They could hear the motorboat pull up. Jansky came into the sub, started the diesel engine, and drove out into the lake. He would not answer any of their questions. After a while, he cut the engine and left the ship without a word. In his place, a large, elderly man appeared through the hatch. He was strong looking, had a flat nose, a pinched mouth, and wore glasses. *He was Willy Steiner, alias Wilhelm Schmidt!*

"I warned you, you pesky kids!" he thundered. "But you didn't listen. Now you're finished!"

"Why don't you give up, Schmidt!" Joe cried out bravely. "You'll never get out of this valley, the police are already on their way!"

"You don't really expect me to fall for that, do you?" Schmidt said derisively. He checked the prisoners' bonds and pulled them tighter, then he stepped up to the controls.

"You've got enough oxygen for half an hour," he declared with a devilish grin. "No one will ever see you or Alfred Wagner's mini-sub again!"

With that, he turned the knob that opened the ballast valves. Then he cut the lights and scurried up through the hatch. The cover fell shut behind him and was sealed from the outside.

Frank and Joe were caught in the slowly sinking submarine!

20 Amphibian Arrest

The boys were almost paralyzed with terror. They began tearing frantically at their bonds, but the ropes only cut deeper into their flesh. They had no time to lose. If the sub crashed to the bottom of the lake, it had little chance of sustaining the shock.

Finally, Frank controlled himself enough to think clearly. "Joe, the toolbox!" he cried out. "Maybe I can reach it!" He wriggled into the right position and, after many unsuccessful attempts, managed to pull out the drawer underneath the seat. Quickly, he felt for a knife, then started to work on Joe's bonds in the dark. The task was made almost impossible by Frank's own tight bonds. But finally he cut the cord, and soon both Hardys were free!

Within seconds, they had closed the ballast valves, started the electric motor, and activated the pump to empty the water tank. They were just in time—the boat was only ten yards above the bottom of the lake!

"Wow!" Frank exclaimed and wiped the perspiration from his forehead. "I'm glad we made it. Do you think the boat would have stayed in one piece after hitting the bottom?"

"I bet it would have been smashed to bits and us along with it," Joe replied. He shuddered at the thought, then took a deep breath. "We'd better get some fresh air before the oxygen runs out."

Cautiously, they ascended. When they reached the surface of the lake, they saw the headlights of a car coming through the woods from the lodge.

Frank unlocked the hatch cover and looked out.

There they go, he thought.

The next moment, the whole forest seemed to come alive! Two shots cracked through the night, shouts were heard, and the headlights went out. Then a maze of flashlights flared up and moved all over.

Frank stared at the scene in amazement. "Joe, the police are here! Let's get going!" he cried out.

Soon they reached the shore and climbed on land. The noise had stopped, and after a few steps, Frank held his brother back by the arm.

"Someone's coming!" he whispered.

A twig rustled, then broke. Tense and alert, the Hardys pressed themselves against an evergreen. They noticed a shadowy figure sneak down to the water's edge about fifteen feet away from them. After a silent signal to each other, they let out a war whoop, jumped the stranger, and pulled him to the ground.

Gerhard Stolz and Detective Schirmer heard their cry and rushed to the scene. "Don't let him get away!" Schirmer exclaimed.

The Hardys took a closer look at their captive. It turned out that the shadowy figure was Wilhelm Schmidt!

"Good work, boys!" Schirmer praised, as he handcuffed the man. "He almost escaped!"

Gerhard put his arms around the young detectives. "Am I glad to see you!" he said. "I was worried when I didn't hear from you, so Sepp and I came up here as fast as we could."

"I'm glad you did," Frank said with a grin.

"How did you catch this guy?" Gerhard went on.

"With the help of *Ludwig II*," Frank responded and pointed to the mini-sub. "We made an amphibian arrest, so to speak."

Everyone laughed, then Joe asked, "What about the other two crooks?"

"They're in custody already," Stolz replied.

"And the paintings?"

"We have them. They even unpacked them for us. As we suspected, the coin collection belonging to Mayor Altenberg was in with them, too!"

"I'm sure Doris will be delighted to get it back," Frank said.

"Why don't we go to the hunting lodge and talk there?" Schirmer suggested and dragged the hand-cuffed prisoner with him.

When they arrived, they found a pot of coffee steaming on the stove, and the two other prisoners under the watchful eye of a police officer.

The Hardys told Gerhard and Detective Schirmer what had happened to them, and the reporter shuddered when he heard how the criminals had intended to get rid of the boys. "That's attempted murder!" he exclaimed. Then he turned angrily to Wilhelm Schmidt. "Steiner, you're going to spend the rest of your life in prison for that!"

"Steiner?" Joe repeated. "That's really Wilhelm Schmidt, the former councilman of Glocken!"

The crook let out a string of curses when Frank explained what they had heard from Heinz.

But no one paid any attention, and Schirmer turned to Jansky. "You may be able to get an easier sentence if you tell us what you know. First of all, how did you ever get into business with Schmidt?"

The man sighed.

"Don't think you owe the Schmidts anything," Frank spoke up. "They were going to get rid of you the minute they didn't need you any longer."

"That's right," Joe added. "We overheard them say so when we eavesdropped here at the window earlier this evening."

"I had a hunch they'd do that!" Jansky stormed. "I was a fool to trust them!"

He had been hired for a huge salary, he now revealed, but had seen little of it. It was not until later that he found out what the Schmidts were up to. By that time, he was so involved that he could not back out.

"Schmidt was obsessed with the treasure in the lake," Jansky went on. "In order to retrieve it, he needed a sub because it was down so deep. And he had to transport the craft to Bear Lake without attracting attention. So he tried to have Lemberg develop one. That would have been the easiest way."

"Oh, now I see why he was so upset when the firm dropped the project," Joe spoke up.

Schirmer looked at Schmidt. "Then you had Tarek steal Wagner's drawings, and you built a copy of *Ludwig II*."

The criminal did not reply.

"As soon as he had retrieved the paintings, he was

going to sabotage Wagner's sub and sell the plans abroad," Jansky revealed.

"Very clever," Gerhard Stolz admitted. "This way he would have killed two birds with one stone."

Jansky nodded. "When he heard from Tarek that Wagner had become suspicious and had asked you for help, he sent Heinz to the garage to give Tarek instructions. Both stood near Wagner's office when the Hardys arrived. Heinz overheard that Stolz was in Glocken, and why. When he told his father about it, Wilhelm sent him after the boys to keep an eye on them."

"He decided to do more than that," Joe said. "He tried to kill us on the Autobahn."

Jansky shrugged. "He happened to catch up with you and took advantage of the opportunity. The interlude with the blond girl reporter had given him the idea of buying the wig, by the way."

"That did confuse us for a while," Frank admitted.

"But when he broke into our hotel room, he made a mistake," Joe added. "That's when we realized the meaning of the Argentinian handkerchief."

"The red Alfa helped, too," Frank said. "It's such a conspicuous car."

Wilhelm Schmidt turned to his son. "You see, what'd I tell you!" he hissed.

"So *you* didn't make any mistakes?" Heinz scoffed. "You left Tarek's note in Stolz's apartment!"

"Shut up!"

Schirmer rubbed his hands together. "Thanks. That explains the attack on Rita Stolz!"

Jansky continued with his story and admitted that Schmidt and he had overpowered Gerhard Stolz and dragged him into the cellar of the house on the lake. Then he had taken Gerhard's Mercedes to the airport and sent the Hardys the telegram. Schmidt had gone to Glocken the same night, where he asked Heinz to scare the young detectives by putting a threatening note on their door. When it did not work, the two set up a trap in the old mine, where Heinz was to lure the boys.

"But that wasn't necessary," the young man said with an evil grin. "They came on their own! I had been there setting the trap when they showed up. I'd call that perfect timing," he added sarcastically.

His father ordered him to be quiet, but Heinz shrugged. "For what? It's all over anyway."

Now he and Jansky both admitted that they had engineered the theft of the truck and the attack in Wagner's workshop. The motorboat with the magnetometer was also stolen but taken to Bear Lake earlier.

"What I don't understand," Gerhard said, "is why the container with the paintings was hidden almost two hundred meters below the surface of the lake!"

"No one planned it that way," Heinz said. "My father had stashed it at the foot of the cliff where there was a small promontory only ten meters deep. But when he wanted to retrieve the treasure, he realized that the landslide had pushed the box way out into the lake."

Schmidt now admitted that during the war he had heard about the investigation Altenberg had started against him, and, being guilty, wanted to avoid punishment. He had managed to exchange identification papers with a dead soldier and sneaked back to Glocken at night without anyone seeing him. He had been familiar with the old mine ever since he was a child and suspected that one of the tunnels led near the Altenbergs' wine cellar. He had dug for weeks to break into the cellar, while his wife supplied him with food.

"And then Fritz Blendinger found out about your scheme, didn't he?" Frank asked.

"H-how did you know?" the criminal stammered. Then, realizing he had nothing to lose, Schmidt admitted that he had killed his former colleague because he was on to him and also took credit for poisoning Altenberg's dog.

After Schmidt had concealed the paintings in Bear Lake, he fled to Argentina, where his wife and son followed. His wife died soon after her arrival. Many years later, Schmidt found a buyer for the paintings and came to Germany.

"That buyer was Braun?" Joe inquired.

"No. I had offered him the pictures, too, but he refused. Now I could have extracted any price from him."

"Why is that?"

"Because he was recently commissioned by a South American collector to buy them," Schmidt replied.

Two days after the capture of the criminals, the Hardys were having coffee and cake with Gerhard and Rita in their Munich apartment, when Sepp Schirmer dropped in.

"I wanted to tell you that Braun confessed," the detective said after pouring himself a steaming cup. "The tip about the surprise at the Glocken ceremony came from him!"

"We wondered about that," Frank said. "But what was his purpose? To confuse us?"

"No. He was hoping the tip would get you on Schmidt's trail and lead you to the paintings. Schmidt had once offered Braun a gold *Joachimstaler*, but had not revealed his name. And he had hinted that he had possession of the paintings. When Braun heard about the public opening of the secret wine cellar in Glocken, he instantly connected Schmidt's story with those pictures. That's why he came to the ceremony."

"So by tipping off Gerhard, he thought Gerhard would be interested in the case, and find the pictures for him, because now he had a customer for them?" Joe asked.

"Right. Then he met Schmidt in the street in Glocken and made a deal with him directly."

Gerhard Stolz grinned. "Well, that winds it up, boys. Now I can write my report for the *Herold*."

"Only it'll be more exciting than you thought, won't it?" Frank said.

Gerhard nodded. "And you and Joe will become international heroes besides getting a ten-thousand-mark reward! By the way, what are you going to do with all that money?"

"I'd like to do some more traveling," Joe suggested. However, he would soon find out that there was no time for travel once he and Frank got involved in a case called *The Four-Headed Dragon*.

You are invited to join

THE OFFICIAL NANCY DREW ®/
HARDY BOYS ® FAN CLUB!

Be the first in your neighborhood to find out
about the newest adventures of Nancy, Frank,
and Joe in the **Nancy Drew** ®/ **Hardy Boys** ®
Mystery Reporter, and to receive your official
membership card. Just send your name, age,
address, and zip code on a postcard *only* to:

The Official Nancy Drew ®/
Hardy Boys ® **Fan Club**
Wanderer Books
Simon & Schuster Building
1230 Avenue of the Americas
New York, New York 10020

THE HARDY BOYS® SERIES
by Franklin W. Dixon

Night of the Werewolf (#59)
Mystery of the Samurai Sword (#60)
The Pentagon Spy (#61)
The Apeman's Secret (#62)
The Mummy Case (#63)
Mystery of Smugglers Cove (#64)
The Stone Idol (#65)
The Vanishing Thieves (#66)
The Outlaw's Silver (#67)
The Submarine Caper (#68)
The Four-Headed Dragon (#69)
The Infinity Clue (#70)

You will also enjoy

THE TOM SWIFT® SERIES
by Victor Appleton

The City in the Stars (#1)
Terror on the Moons of Jupiter (#2)
The Alien Probe (#3)
The War in Outer Space (#4)
The Astral Fortress (#5)
The Rescue Mission (#6)